THREE SCREENPLAYS

Jean Cocteau

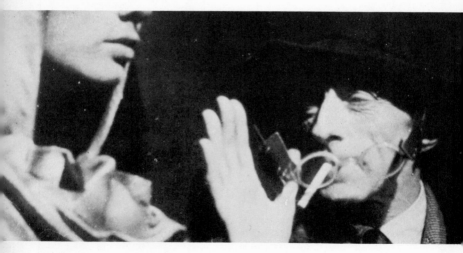

THREE SCREENPLAYS

L' Eternel Retour

Orphée

La Belle et la Bête

Translated from the French by Carol Martin-Sperry

Grossman Publishers New York 1972

L'Eternel Retour, Orphée, La Belle et la Bête
English language translation Copyright © 1972 by The Viking Press, Inc.
All rights reserved
First published in 1972 in a hardbound and paperbound edition by
Grossman Publishers
625 Madison Avenue, New York, N.Y. 10022
Published simultaneously in Canada by
Fitzhenry and Whiteside, Ltd.
SBN 670-22664-5 (hardbound)
SBN 670-22665-3 (paperbound)
Library of Congress Catalogue Card Number: 78-138258
Printed in U.S.A.

CONTENTS

L'Eternel Retour   *(1943)*

Credits

Screenplay and dialogue	Jean Cocteau
Director	Jean Delannoy
Producer	André Paulvé
Music	Georges Auric
Cast:	
Natalie	Madeleine Sologne
Patrice	Jean Marais
Gertrude	Yvone de Bray
Marc	Jean Murat
Natalie II	Junie Astor
Lionel	Roland Toutain
Achille	Pieral
Anne	Jeanne Marken
Amédée	Jean d'Yd
Morolt	Alexandre Rignault

Marc, an extremely rich man who owns vast estates, lives in a magnificent 17th-century castle. At first there are no indications that we are in the 20th century. He lives with his nephew, Patrice, and the strange family of his deceased wife, the Frossins: his sister-in-law, Gertrude; her crotchety old husband, Amédée; and their dwarf son, Achille. The latter, who displays a deep hatred for both beings and objects, has just killed the gardener's dog. Claude, the gardener, crosses the courtyard at a gloomy pace. He is carrying a bundle in his arms but is too far away for one to make out what it is. Gertrude appears at a window in the tower.

GERTRUDE *(shouting):* Achille! . . . Achille! . . . *(Receiving no reply, she turns to Claude.)* Claude . . . have you seen Master Achille?

Claude looks up toward the balcony with a tragic expression on his face.

CLAUDE: Here he is, your Achille . . . here's what he's done, your Achille.

Claude is holding a dead dog in his arms. Its bloody head is hanging down.

GERTRUDE: My God!

She disappears from the window; Claude carries off his dead dog.

Corridors. Patrice's room.

Gertrude wanders through the corridors looking for Achille. Achille listens, hidden behind a door.

GERTRUDE *(moving away):* Achille! . . . Achille!

Achille looks around with a sly expression. He goes into Patrice's room and stops in front of a table that has Patrice's portrait standing on it. He knocks down the portrait with his fist. There is an open pack of cigarettes on another table. He takes it. He opens the closet and takes out one of the ties hanging inside.

GERTRUDE *(coming nearer):* Achille! . . . Achille!

Achille flattens himself against the wall and listens. Gertrude, who is tired of looking for him, goes back to her apartment.

The Frossins' apartment.

Amédée is sitting at a long, narrow table that is laden with all kinds of firearms. He is busy cleaning the parts of an almost entirely dismantled gun. Gertrude enters. She is very angry.

GERTRUDE: Bravo! Let me congratulate you! You've really done it this time!

AMÉDÉE: What?

GERTRUDE: I've told you over and over again that it's insane to collect firearms and to handle them in front of Achille.

AMÉDÉE: But I never use them!

GERTRUDE: Those stupid arms would give anyone murderous thoughts . . . *(She turns toward Amédée and talks in an ominously calm voice.)* Achille has killed Claude's dog! He shot it.

Amédée's expression changes. He stands up and looks from Gertrude to the guns.

AMÉDÉE: With one of my guns? *(He hurries toward the racks.)* He stole one of my guns? *(Amédée strokes his guns.)*

GERTRUDE: Is that all you care about? *(She holds her head in her hands.)* I shall go mad . . . mad!

Amédée does not react. He continues checking his collection. He becomes calmer.

AMÉDÉE: There's not a single one missing!

Gertrude flops down in an armchair.

GERTRUDE *(to herself):* . . . He killed Claude's dog . . . Still another fuss with Marc. Where can the child be?

AMÉDÉE: Achille is not a child.

GERTRUDE *(sitting up straight):* Achille is not a child?

AMÉDÉE *(returning to his work):* No . . . he's a dwarf.

GERTRUDE: Amédée!

Amédée is cleaning the barrel of a gun, looking through it from time to time.

AMÉDÉE: A twenty-four-year-old dwarf. We have a twenty-four-year-old son who is a dwarf. And each time you treat him like a child you provoke him . . . I'm taking the liberty of pointing this out to you.

GERTRUDE: Is it my fault that the wretched child is a dwarf?

AMÉDÉE: It's certainly not my fault.

GERTRUDE: Well! Do I look like a dwarf to you?

AMÉDÉE: You're not very tall . . .

GERTRUDE: That's marvelous! As though that had anything to do with it . . . not very tall! . . . And what about your hunch-backed great-grandfather? What do you say to that?

AMÉDÉE: Nothing; I admit it.

GERTRUDE: You should think before you speak, my dear. Achille is my son. Don't you forget that. And I adore him.

Amédée listens carefully, then signals Gertrude to be quiet and points to the door.

AMÉDÉE: Gertrude!

GERTRUDE: What is it?

They both stare at the door. The handle turns silently. They whisper.

AMÉDÉE: Achille . . . he's eavesdropping.

GERTRUDE: My God! . . . I hope he didn't hear anything, the poor little thing!

Without saying a word, they move away from each other. Gertrude sits down in an armchair and concentrates on reading a magazine. Amédée returns to his work, with his back to the door. The door opens slowly. Achille enters and looks ironically at his mother and father. He walks across the room.

GERTRUDE *(affectionately):* Where've you been, dear?

ACHILLE: Nowhere . . .

AMÉDÉE: Your mother's asking you where you've been.

GERTRUDE: Leave the child alone, Amédée.

AMÉDÉE: Fine, fine.

ACHILLE: I'm no longer a child. And don't you forget it.

GERTRUDE: Of course, my darling! . . . Come and kiss me. *(Achille ungraciously goes over to his mother and offers her his cheek.)* Are you sulking?

Gertrude leans forward to hug and kiss him. Suddenly she notices Achille's pocket. One end of the stolen tie is hanging out. Without letting go of him, Gertrude moves her hand around and grabs the tie. Achille is aware of his mother's movement. He leaps back. The tie unfolds in Gertrude's hand.

GERTRUDE: What's this?

ACHILLE: It's a tie!

GERTRUDE: Do you think I'm an idiot? Whose tie is it?

AMÉDÉE: Your mother's asking you whose tie it is.

Achille, with a sly look, does not answer.

GERTRUDE: Is it one of Patrice's ties?

ACHILLE: Yes.

Gertrude stands up. Achille instinctively moves back.

GERTRUDE: You stole it from his room? *(She walks toward him.)* Come closer, closer . . .

Gertrude is still walking toward Achille, who is retreating.

AMÉDÉE *(weakly):* Your mother wants you to come closer.

GERTRUDE: What do you have in your pockets? . . . Come on now, show me!

Achille is furious but is overcome by his mother. He takes out several objects from his pockets and puts them on the table: a car plug, a suggestive post card, a doorknob, a dead bird. Regretfully, he pulls out a pack of cigarettes and puts it on the table.

GERTRUDE: You're going to put that tie back at once . . . at once, do you hear me? *(Achille does not move. Gertrude comes toward him.)* Do you want me to hit you? *(Achille retreats.)*

AMÉDÉE: Gertrude!

Gertrude goes up to Achille, who protects himself with his arm.

GERTRUDE: Do you want me to hit you?

Achille is by the window. Gertrude is about to hit him but, at that very moment, notices something outside. She leaves Achille and goes to the window.

The courtyard.

Patrice rides up on his white horse. His dog, Moulouk, is barking behind him. He stops at the foot of the steps, jumps down from his horse, and takes a quick look at the Frossins' window. They are all staring out. As soon as Patrice raises his eyes to the window, the three faces vanish. Patrice smiles, goes gaily up the steps, and talks to Moulouk.

PATRICE: Moulouk, you saw them, weren't you afraid?

He disappears into the castle.

The Frossins' apartment.

The three Frossins are still waiting in ambush at the window.

AMÉDÉE: He saw us.

GERTRUDE: So what? Aren't we allowed to look out the window? ... There you are, Achille, you see what happens when you start to argue ... Go to your cousin as though you just wanted to say good morning to him and find a way to put the tie back in its place. *(She gives him the tie and the pack of cigarettes.)* I hope you're big enough ... *(correcting herself)* I mean, I hope you're intelligent enough to understand that we cannot allow the slightest thing to be held against us ... in a house that doesn't belong to us.

ACHILLE *(like a child):* Yes, mommy.

AMÉDÉE: Don't be insolent to your mother.

ACHILLE *(in the same way):* Yes, daddy.

He walks away, throwing an evil look at his parents. He leaves the room, whistling and dragging his hand across the furniture.

Patrice's room.

Patrice is carrying his dog on his shoulders. He throws him down and holds out his arms.

PATRICE: Here, here ... come here ... *(The dog leaps into his arms. There is a knock on the door. Patrice, still holding the dog in his arms, turns toward the door.)* Come in! *(Achille appears, with a friendly expression.)* Ah, it's you. What can I do for you?

Achille comes in and takes a few steps.

ACHILLE: Nothing ... I just wanted to say hello ...

PATRICE: How kind ... Moulouk, say hello. *(He puts the dog down.)*

ACHILLE: Don't bother. Your dog hates me. *(He moves away.)*

PATRICE: Well then, he'll bite you! *(laughing and joking)* Bite him, Moulouk! Bite him! Bite him!

ACHILLE: Patrice!

Achille, chased by Patrice and Moulouk, pretends to be frightened but, instead of retreating toward the door, goes toward the closet. The dog barks. When Achille reaches the closet he opens the door and hides behind it.

PATRICE: Behind the mirror, Moulouk, behind the mirror, jump ... go on! Bite him!

Hidden behind the mirror, Achille suddenly drops his frightened expression but continues to shout.

ACHILLE *(shouting):* Fool! You stupid fool! ... Patrice!

While he is shouting he takes out the tie and puts it back in its place.

PATRICE: But you know that Moulouk never bites anyone! Come out of the closet.

Achille slides halfway out from behind the closet.

ACHILLE: Hold back that foul beast or I'll scream.

PATRICE: Scream, scream, my dear boy! ... Go on, Moulouk! Go on, bite him! Bite him! ...

Achille rushes toward the door. He opens it quickly and escapes. He dashes down the corridor at top speed, looks behind him, and stops. Reassured, he tears at his pocket, ruffles his hair, and puts on a tearful face.

ACHILLE *(shouting):* Mommy! Mommy!

The door opens. Gertrude is there. Achille rushes toward her.

GERTRUDE: Oh, darling, what's the matter? ... What have they done to you? ...

ACHILLE *(sobbing):* The dog ... the dog ... Patrice made him bite me.

The courtyard.

A car drives through the grounds and stops in front of the steps. Marc gets out. Claude, the gardener, comes to the car and starts to take out the baggage.

MARC *(to Claude):* Leave that, Claude, Maurice will take care of it. *(He holds the suitcase out to the chauffeur.)* Everyone all right?

CLAUDE: Well ... I don't like it when my Lord goes away, even for three days ...

Marc notices Claude's upset expression.

MARC: What's wrong? ... *(pauses)* Master Achille?

CLAUDE: Yes, sir ... but my Lord will hear about it soon enough ...

Claude turns away. Marc, looking thoughtful, goes into the house.

The dining room.

Gertrude is sitting at the table. The meal is almost over. The atmosphere is icy. Gertrude tries to look calm, but one can sense that she is wound up, ready to spring. She is finishing a pear with a falsely nonchalant air. Every now and then she throws a sharp look around her. Achille catches his mother's eye and looks down at his plate. Amédée is drinking with a detached expression in an attempt to conceal his embarrassment. He coughs.

Patrice is busy feeding sugar to Moulouk, who has put his paws on his master's knees.

GERTRUDE: That dog doesn't deserve any sugar.

PATRICE: Why not, dear Aunt?

MARC: What a strange dinner . . . what's the matter with you all? Is it because I've returned?

Achille stares at his plate.

GERTRUDE: It's just that the dog has bitten Achille.

ACHILLE: Oh, mommy! . . .

GERTRUDE: Be quiet! Patrice excited the dog on purpose till it bit him.

PATRICE: Uncle Marc, Moulouk never bites anyone . . .

GERTRUDE: Am I lying? Achille! . . .

Achille suddenly gets up, throws down his napkin, and disappears.

MARC *(wearily, to Gertrude):* If you don't mind, I'd rather we didn't talk about dogs any more tonight.

GERTRUDE *(stiffening):* And why not?

Amédée, who is very embarrassed, tries to hold her back. He makes a conciliatory gesture.

MARC: Because you will cause me to lose my temper. I must ask you to keep an eye on Achille.

GERTRUDE: What are you accusing him of?

Amédée looks at the ceiling, wondering how far Gertrude will go.

MARC: Listen, Gertrude, it's wrong of you to insist, very wrong. *(Amédée nods in approval.)*

GERTRUDE *(shaking):* Of course! I'm always wrong ... *(Amédée closes his eyes and hunches his shoulders.)* For years now I've always been wrong, just as my charming sisters were always right.

MARC: Edith and Solange are dead, Gertrude; let them lie in peace.

GERTRUDE: Very convenient! No ... no ... Edith was always right because she was your wife ... Solange was always right because she was Patrice's mother ... and I'm always wrong because I'm Achille's mother. *(She bursts into tears.)* I wish I were dead!

MARC: Gertrude ... Gertrude!

GERTRUDE: Leave me alone! It's dreadful. A poor child who suffers because he's not like the others ... a poor child who ... oh! oh! ... *(She chokes on her tears.)*

MARC *(sighing):* Patrice, come up to my study, I want to talk to you.

Marc leaves the room, followed by Patrice and Moulouk. Gertrude is sobbing. Amédée goes up to her.

AMÉDÉE: Come now, my dear.

Gertrude straightens up.

GERTRUDE: Oh! you ... Leave me alone! *(moaning)* Achille ... Achille ... I wish I were dead ... dead! ...

She gets up and leaves the room. The door slams behind her. Amédée remains, alone.

Marc's study.

Marc has just entered his study. Patrice closes the door behind him.
They both go toward Marc's desk . . . talking as they walk. Moulouk
is with them . . .

MARC *(wearily):* I so dislike this business. Achille shot Claude's dog
with a rifle.

PATRICE: How dreadful!

MARC: Achille is a disaster. *(Marc sits down at his desk.)* I wanted to
be alone with you for a while.

PATRICE: Uncle Marc, you look absolutely exhausted.

MARC: Your aunt and your mother helped me tolerate their sister's
scenes. I admit that I'm finding it more and more difficult to put
up with her now.

PATRICE: Since everyone we ever loved died at sea, Gertrude ought
to be happy.

MARC: Don't be unfair. What do you expect, she is suffering. She
saw my despair. She saw that I was bringing you up like a son.
She sees you.

PATRICE: She sees only a little of me. I'm almost always out on the
land, and I'd like to be of more help to you. *(Marc stands up*
and walks in front of Patrice, who follows him with his eyes.)
Dear uncle . . . *(Marc has just walked past Patrice. He stops*
and turns around.) You shouldn't be living alone.

MARC: But I have you, Patrice.

PATRICE: Oh! me . . . No, what's missing here is a woman.

MARC: Well, now!

PATRICE: They think I'm monopolizing you. If you remarried, it
would be the greatest trick you could play on them.

MARC *(smiling):* But whom could I marry, my dear Patrice? A lady
from the neighborhood?

PATRICE: A young girl.

MARC *(laughing):* No young girl would want me.

PATRICE: You are much younger than I, Uncle Marc ... Uncle Marc, tell me to find you a young girl and I'll find her for you. *(Patrice, in his enthusiasm, walks around Marc, and finally grabs him by the arm. Marc laughs at his eagerness.)* And she'll be the youngest and the most beautiful. And she'll love you and you'll love her. And they'll burst with jealousy!

They stop by the door.

MARC *(laughing, to Patrice):* Go on, then, look for her ... look for her, Moulouk! *(Moulouk pricks his ears.)*

PATRICE: Is that a challenge? I shall look for her and I shall bring her back.

Marc makes a sign at Patrice that means "With your permission." He goes to the door and opens it, suddenly. Achille, caught by surprise, runs away, holding his shoes in his hand.

MARC: What a charming family! Are you going to the island tomorrow?

PATRICE: Yes, my Lord, and I shall torment your serfs ...

MARC: I only ask them to pay what they owe.

PATRICE: Goodnight, Uncle Marc.

MARC: Goodnight, you madman!

Patrice leaves the room. Marc remains on the doorstep.

The sea.

Patrice is sitting in the front of a motorboat. Moulouk is beside him. A dark flag flies from the top of the mast. It is evening. The island is near.

The little harbor.

The boat stops alongside a small jetty. Patrice and Moulouk jump out. Jules, the owner of the boat, hands Patrice's bag to him.

PATRICE: Goodnight, Jules; I'll send you a message when I want to return.

Patrice climbs up some steps that lead to a badly-lit alley. He follows the alley. Suddenly, a glass smashes against the wall next to him. The wall is splattered with wine. Patrice stops and notices that the missile came from a sailors' hangout, the Velo Bar. Inside, one can hear laughter and Morolt's voice. The entrance to the bar consists of two low swinging doors. The glass had been thrown out over the top.

In the doorway, a woman and a small child are huddled against the frame, out of the line of fire. Once again there is the sound of breaking glass and Morolt's laughter.

PATRICE *(to the woman):* What's going on?

THE WOMAN: It's always the same fellow. *(Patrice goes nearer to the door and takes a look.)* Don't go in! He's drunk . . . and when he's drunk he's dangerous . . .

Patrice, his head and shoulders showing above the door, looks in. It is a bar, tobacco shop, and general store all in one. There are several tables occupied by local fishermen and peasants. Most are silent; some pretend to laugh at Morolt's jokes. He is standing near the bar, almost as big as a giant. He is drunk and has decided to clean off all the glasses that are cluttering up the bar. The owner and the barmaid are very wisely standing behind the bar. They have weak smiles on their faces. The owner is surreptitiously trying to remove the remaining glasses. But Morolt is aware of this. He pushes back the owner, grabs another glass, and aims at the door.

MOROLT: Leave me alone! Leave me alone!

Patrice lowers his head, thereby avoiding the glass, which smashes against the wall in the street. He enters the bar. A huge laugh from Morolt. Patrice walks toward the counter. Morolt grabs another glass.

MOROLT: Look! Oh! wait a minute — ah!

This time he takes aim in the room itself. The glass and its contents smash against the wall. Just below, three men sitting at a table lower their heads. When the scare is over they laugh weakly. They are all cowards. Morolt, standing against the bar, takes no notice of Patrice, who is leaning on the counter some distance away. Morolt picks up another glass. The owner tries to take it from him.

MOROLT: Leave me alone!

Morolt throws the glass in the room. It smashes against the wall

*above a young blonde who is sitting alone, away from the others.
This is Natalie. Morolt laughs. Natalie closes her eyes. She opens
them again and gets up, looking straight ahead. She goes toward
Morolt, passing the others who are still laughing.*

NATALIE: Stop it, Morolt!

MOROLT: Leave me alone!

NATALIE: Come on, Morolt, it's time to go home . . .

MOROLT: Leave me alone! Drink. *(He hands her a glass of red wine.
She shakes her head.)* Come on! Drink!

NATALIE: No, Morolt. Let's go!

MOROLT: Leave me alone!

*He puts down the glass, grabs Natalie by the arm, holds her against
the counter, and tries to force her to drink. He takes her by her hair
and pushes her head down onto the counter. He accidentally knocks
over the glass.*

MOROLT: Drink . . . well now, drink . . . drink! Come on!

NATALIE: Stop it, Morolt. Stop it.

Morolt rubs Natalie's head in a puddle of wine on the counter.

MOROLT *(laughing):* Leave me alone!

*Patrice puts his hand on Morolt's arm. The laughter stops. Morolt
lets go of Natalie and turns around. Patrice looks at him calmly.
Morolt snickers. Natalie is behind Morolt and, as she passes her
hand over his dirty face, she signals to Patrice: "Don't say anything,
let him be; don't get mixed up in this." Patrice is leaning against the
counter.*

PATRICE *(to the owner):* A brandy.

THE OWNER: A brandy — yes, sir.

Morolt stares at him and snickers. The incident has sobered him.

The thought of a fight excites him. He grabs the bottle from the owner, picks up the glass he had knocked over, fills it, and, without taking his eyes off Patrice, speaks to Natalie.

MOROLT: Drink it.

Natalie looks around, trying to calculate how dangerous it would be to refuse. She looks like a hunted animal. Then, overcome, she goes up to the counter between the two men. She takes the glass with an obvious repulsion and brings it to her lips. But Patrice puts his hand on the glass. Natalie is forced to put it down on the counter. She steps back. Morolt, quite sobered by his anger, points to the glass, still without taking his eyes off Patrice.

MOROLT *(to Natalie):* Drink it!

As Natalie puts out her hand, Patrice, still looking Morolt straight in the eye, stops her.

PATRICE: No.

MOROLT *(getting angrier):* Drink it!

PATRICE: No.

Morolt's fist lashes out. Natalie screams. Patrice dodges and throws a blow with his right, hitting Morolt on the chin. Morolt falls back onto a table, which smashes to bits. The men who were sitting at the table push each other back in confusion.

Various shouts. Moulouk, held by a fisherman, barks. Natalie, terrified, watches Morolt as he stands up. When he is on his feet again he advances menacingly toward Patrice. He takes a deep breath and lunges at him with lowered head. Patrice receives the blow full force and falls down, while Morolt, carried away by his speed, goes right over Patrice and hits the wall head-on. He falls, stunned. Notebooks, pencils, and boxes clatter down around him. Patrice drags himself up with some difficulty and leans against the counter. He grabs Natalie by the arm.

PATRICE: Don't stay here . . . come on . . .

Morolt lifts his head, shakes himself, and gropes for something in his pocket. Patrice tries to pull Natalie away but he is forced to cling to the counter for support, and Natalie has to come to his assistance.

NATALIE: Watch out!

Morolt has opened his knife. He throws it at Patrice. Patrice's face contracts with pain. The knife is embedded up to the hilt in his thigh.

Morolt stands up and staggers to the bar. Blood is flowing from his forehead. He drags himself over to Patrice, knocking down bottles on his way. They are both clinging to the counter, their legs too weak to hold them. Patrice seizes a bottle from the counter, lifts it, and smashes it down on Morolt's skull. Morolt collapses, bringing Patrice down with him.

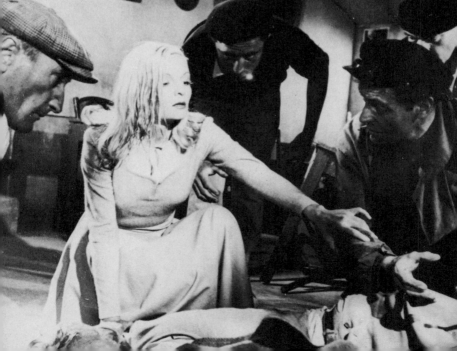

The two men, unconscious, fall on top of one another. People approach them with new-found courage and lean over them, giving advice.

NATALIE *(kneeling down):* Don't pull the knife out, it's dangerous. Bring him to my home . . . quickly . . .

Four men hoist Patrice up onto their shoulders and take him out; Natalie follows. Her face is near Patrice's head, which is hanging down. She holds up his head.

Anne's room.

A simple and clean peasant's room. The bed is in a corner against the wall. The morning sun is shining through the window. The curtains are waving in the breeze. Patrice is sleeping. Anne, sitting by the bed, watches over him. The door opens; Natalie appears.

NATALIE: He still doesn't look very well, does he?

Anne looks at Patrice, who is still asleep.

ANNE: I've been giving him herbs to lower the fever. In three days it'll be over. *(They both look at Patrice.)* He's handsome.

NATALIE: It's not a face from the neighborhood.

Anne leaves the room. Natalie moves closer to Patrice. She takes his hand ... He opens his eyes. She quickly draws back her hand. Patrice looks at her.

NATALIE: Don't talk.

PATRICE: Talking isn't tiring. It's moving my head that's tiring.

He has taken her hand and he makes her sit down on the edge of the bed.

NATALIE: You're lucky that Anne has the gift of healing and knows all about herbs.

PATRICE: Who's Anne?

NATALIE: She brought me up. My parents were Norwegian. They had a boat. They left on a cruise just after I was born on this island. The doctor didn't want them to take me with them. The boat was shipwrecked.

PATRICE: Were your parents drowned?

NATALIE: Yes.

PATRICE: So were mine. We are children of the sea. *(pauses)* What does that Morolt mean to you?

NATALIE: He's going to marry me and then he'll kill me.

PATRICE: You're engaged to that drunkard?

NATALIE: He seems to think so.

PATRICE: How old are you?

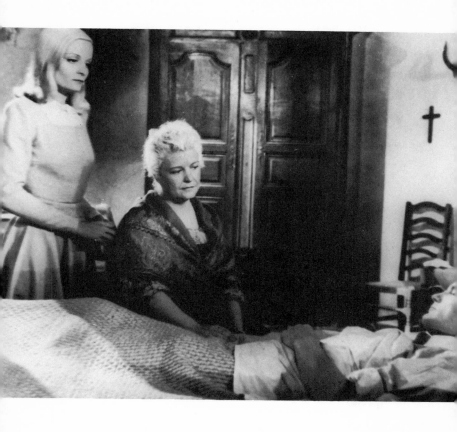

NATALIE: My name's Natalie. I'm twenty-two.

PATRICE: I'm twenty-four. My name's Patrice.

Anne's room. Several days later.

Patrice is standing, leaning against the window sill. Moulouk is lying at the foot of the bed. Footsteps are heard coming up the stairs. Patrice turns around. He listens, and then, like a child caught doing something he shouldn't, goes back to the bed and lies down. The door opens.

PATRICE *(without seeing who it is):* Anne, is that you?

NATALIE: No, it's Natalie. *(She goes up to Patrice.)* Are you feeling better?

PATRICE: Well ... yes! But I don't feel very strong standing up ... If you didn't walk Moulouk, I think he'd be more ill than his master ...

Moulouk puts his paws on the edge of the bed. Natalie strokes his head.

NATALIE: I shall miss him ...

PATRICE: Are you throwing me out?

NATALIE: You're not from the island. You're well now. Anne gave up her room for you. You'll go home and this affair with the knife will seem like a bad dream.

PATRICE: You're not from the island either.

NATALIE: Oh! me . . .

Patrice props himself up on his elbow and talks without daring to look at Natalie.

PATRICE: Wouldn't you like to leave the island, Morolt, the bad dream? . . . Wouldn't you like to escape from all this, on the quiet? . . . Cross the water, marry a man worthy of you, and live? . . . *(Natalie is overwhelmed. The tears well up; she cries, without moving her head.)* You're not really living here . . . you're dead . . . you would have a castle . . . a car . . . servants, trees, roads, animals, money . . . love. *(Patrice is completely unaware that Natalie has turned around, leaning against the bed, her head slightly thrown back. He continues talking, without looking at her.)* You're very intimidating, you know . . . I've got to take my courage in both hands to make this absurd proposition to you . . . *(He turns his head toward her but can see only her profile. He sits up on his knees and turns around.)* You're crying?

She turns toward him with a strange expression.

NATALIE: No, I'm not crying . . . .

She turns around. Patrice takes her by the shoulders.

PATRICE *(gaily):* Listen, Natalie, listen to me. Will you listen to me? . . . There. I have an uncle who looks younger than any of us and who is a very worthy man . . . *(Natalie listens.)* and I want . . . well, that is . . . I would like you . . . to become his wife. *(A shadow passes over Natalie's face.)* Natalie . . . *(a pause)* Natalie! *(Natalie frees herself and suddenly leaves him.)* What's wrong? . . . Natalie . . . Answer me . . .

Natalie leaves the room; the door slams shut behind her.

The ground floor.

Natalie comes down the stairs. She crosses the hall, opens the door, and stops. Morolt has just appeared in the doorway. He is carrying a club. Natalie moves back to the table. Morolt enters the room and closes the door without taking his eyes off her.

NATALIE: What are you doing here?

MOROLT: I've come to settle a little matter . . . *(He glances upward.)* . . . Is he up there?

Natalie sits down on a chair.

NATALIE: Yes . . . he's up there . . . go on up.

Morolt is somewhat taken aback by her attitude. He goes to the staircase and stops, hesitating. Natalie watches him.

NATALIE *(almost violently):* Well then, go on up . . .

Morolt turns around and looks at her.

MOROLT: Does it bother you?

Natalie shrugs her shoulders.

NATALIE: Me . . . I couldn't care less.

Morolt goes up a few steps with a determined air. Then he stops and talks to her over the banister.

MOROLT: You'd like to protect him, wouldn't you?

Natalie leans back against the table and takes her time before answering.

NATALIE: You really are stupid, Morolt.

Morolt comes back down the stairs.

MOROLT: Talk then, since you're so intelligent.

NATALIE: I thought our marriage was a matter we had agreed upon.

Morolt steps off the last stair. He goes up to Natalie.

MOROLT: So?

NATALIE: So, we're not going to get married between two policemen.

MOROLT: I'd like to smash his face in.

He leans toward her. She gets up calmly.

NATALIE: Settle your affair afterward and don't make a scene in Anne's house ... *(She turns toward him and points upward.)* The whole island belongs to his uncle. Do you understand?

MOROLT: Well then, let him get the hell out of here.

NATALIE: He's leaving tomorrow. Then we'll be at ease and we'll get married.

Morolt puts his arm around her. Their faces are very near each other.

MOROLT: You mean it?

NATALIE: I mean it.

MOROLT: And if I killed him you wouldn't mind?

NATALIE: Me? I hate him. You have all the time in the world to settle the affair.

MOROLT: Well then, throw him out.

NATALIE: Tomorrow.

MOROLT: Agreed?

NATALIE: Agreed.

He is about to kiss her, but she breaks away from him, opens the door, and shows him out.

NATALIE: Go now.

Morolt hesitates, looks regretfully in the direction of the stairs, gets ready to leave, and turns around in the doorway.

MOROLT: All the same . . . I would have liked to smash his face in . . .

Natalie closes the door behind him and leans wearily against the wall. Then she goes upstairs.

Anne's room.

Patrice is sitting on the edge of the bed, stroking Moulouk. Natalie enters and closes the door behind her. Patrice gets up at once and comes toward her.

PATRICE: Why did you run away?

Natalie comes forward with a composed expression. One cannot read anything on her face.

NATALIE: I thought you were making fun of me . . . it was stupid of me.

She walks past Patrice without looking at him.

PATRICE: Well then?

NATALIE: Well what?

PATRICE: You haven't given me an answer.

NATALIE: Why would your uncle want to marry me?

PATRICE: Because as soon as he sees you he will fall in love with you. Do you accept?

NATALIE *(after a pause):* Yes, I accept.

PATRICE: I knew I'd be lucky! I must talk to you about Uncle Marc and tell you about the family.

Natalie cuts short Patrice's enthusiasm.

NATALIE: You can tell me on the way. We must leave tonight. *(She goes toward the door.)*

PATRICE: But that's impossible . . .

Natalie turns around.

NATALIE: I know a fisherman who will take us. Wait for me at the promontory. I'll meet you there in an hour.

She leaves the room.

The ground floor.

Anne is pouring some liquid into a flask. Pots are cooking on the stove. Natalie comes down the stairs. She is wearing a long cape and is ready to leave. There is a suitcase on the table.

NATALIE: Has he gone?

ANNE: Yes.

Anne goes toward Natalie and corks the flask. The two women look at each other.

NATALIE: It makes me sad to leave you, Anne.

ANNE: Are you going to marry his uncle?

NATALIE: I've had enough of being poor.

ANNE: And . . . do you think you'll love this uncle?

NATALIE: It doesn't matter. I want to leave the island.

As she says this, Anne takes the bag from the table and slips in the flask.

ANNE: You think it doesn't matter? I don't agree with you.

NATALIE: What are you doing?

ANNE *(like a child caught doing something she shouldn't)*: Listen, my little one . . . I want to ask you something.

Natalie takes the flask and looks at it with a smile. It is labeled "Poison."

ANNE: The label's so that no one touches it.

NATALIE *(nodding her head):* **Now,** what is it?

ANNE: Laugh at me, I don't care. It's an herbal wine. Those who drink it love each other all their lives and forever after.

NATALIE: My poor Anne . . . I don't believe in your herbs.

ANNE: Be happy and promise me that . . .

Natalie takes her in her arms.

NATALIE *(laughing):* I don't believe in it, but I promise. *(She moves away and looks at the flask again before putting it in her bag.)* I like the label. It'll look as though I'm poisoning my husband and myself.

The promontory.

In the last glow of the setting sun, Natalie comes up to a small jetty at the edge of the rocks. A fisherman is waiting there with a boat. Patrice gives his hand to Natalie and helps her down. They sit down next to each other in the stern, and the boat heads out to sea. Natalie, her hair streaming in the wind, looks straight ahead. Patrice is watching her stealthily. One feels that he wants to say something to her but does not dare.

PATRICE *(firmly):* Natalie, there's something else I must tell you. *(Natalie is silent.)* You'll think I'm ludicrous, I know. When you left my room and slammed the door behind you, and I was alone, I thought . . . *(Natalie remains silent.)* . . . Well, I was foolish enough to think . . . that you had believed I wasn't talking about my uncle . . . but about myself . . .

NATALIE: You're just like a child . . .

Marc's castle appears, set in the beautiful countryside. Patrice is on horseback, holding Natalie in front of him.

NATALIE: Can you see me living in that castle?

PATRICE *(closing his eyes):* Yes, I can.

NATALIE: Patrice, take me back to the island.

PATRICE: Hold on tight.

The horse climbs up a long, grassy slope.

The courtyard.

Marc is standing on the steps, watching Patrice and Natalie as they arrive. Patrice stops the horse a few yards away from him. Marc walks down the steps and goes up to them. Patrice helps Natalie slide slowly down to the ground. Natalie looks at Marc. He is stunned by this apparition.

PATRICE *(introducing them):* Uncle Marc . . . Natalie . . .

Without taking his eyes off her, Marc takes the young girl's hand.

The Frossins' apartment.

Achille, armed with a pair of scissors, is concentrating on a very delicate operation.

In the background, Amédée is sitting at his table, sorting out some papers.

AMÉDÉE: What are you doing?

ACHILLE: I'm making ties for the flies.

AMÉDÉE: That's ridiculous!

Achille has completed his operation. He goes to the window and frees the fly. He holds onto the window sill and leans out.

ACHILLE: Oh!

AMÉDÉE: What is it? *(silence from Achille)* You might answer when you're spoken to.

ACHILLE: It's Patrice with a lady, and Uncle Marc has taken her by the hand.

AMÉDÉE: What are you talking about?

Amédée gets up and goes toward the window.

ACHILLE: Take a look for yourself. No one ever believes me.

Amédée leans out the window. In the background Gertrude crosses the room. She is wearing a dressing gown and is rubbing cream on her face.

AMÉDÉE: Gertrude!

GERTRUDE: What's going on? *(She leans out between Achille and Amédée, with cream still all over her face. All three stand up.)* Now what's going on?

Natalie's room.

Patrice is showing the room to Natalie. Natalie is by the window.

PATRICE: View over the grounds ... you can hear the frogs ... Uncle Marc lives above you. *(He turns around. The room has been prepared for Natalie. Patrice continues explaining and shows her the staircase.)* The staircase leads up to his room. He occupies the whole right-hand corner. Do you like Uncle Marc?

NATALIE: He seems very kind.

PATRICE: You've yet to meet the clowns. *(Patrice goes toward the bathroom.)* And here is your bathroom. *(He stops in front of a medicine cabinet and opens it.)* Your medicine cabinet. For snake bites ... mosquito bites ... family bites ... *(He picks up a little bottle.)* ... not forgetting the cure for bicycle falls, bruises *(He sniffs the bottle.)* ... ah, my childhood! *(He replaces the bottle.)* I'll let you rest. They'll bring you everything you need. Tomorrow we'll go into town with the Ford to get whatever else you may want ... *(They stop near the door.)* Are you happy?

Patrice opens the door. Achille, who was eavesdropping, runs away. Natalie cries out.

NATALIE: Oh!

Patrice and Natalie watch the dwarf as he runs away. Patrice makes a sign to Natalie, meaning "You see what I mean?"

NATALIE: But Patrice, tell me, is he really a dwarf?

PATRICE: His mother thinks he's very tall for a dwarf. But there can be no doubt; he's a dwarf. You'll see, you'll get used to it.

He leaves the room.

The hallway.

Marc is going up the stairs. He is lost in thought and does not notice Gertrude, who is on her way down to meet him. As he passes her without saying a word, she stops.

GERTRUDE: Are you sleepwalking?

Marc stops, two steps above her, as though in a dream. He is still stunned by the apparition of Natalie. There is a continual smile on his lips.

MARC *(friendly):* Excuse me, I was thinking.

GERTRUDE: What's going on?

MARC: Nothing.

GERTRUDE: Are there guests coming?

MARC: No, no . . . Patrice has brought a friend to stay for a few days. He's showing her her room.

GERTRUDE *(shocked):* Edith's room?

MARC: I don't want that room to remain dead.

He continues up the stairs. Gertrude looks at him sharply.

GERTRUDE *(after a short pause):* And this friend of Patrice's is just . . . a friend?

MARC: Just a friend.

The drawing room. After dinner.

They are all sitting around a wood fire burning in the huge fireplace. Marc is seated in a large armchair; Gertrude is working at a piece of tapestry. At her feet, Achille is teasing the cat with the poker. There is a heavy silence. Natalie and Patrice laugh. Three heads immediately turn toward them. Silence once more. A new burst of laughter from Natalie and Patrice. They are playing chess.

NATALIE: I'll never learn how to play chess.

PATRICE: You're not paying attention.

Marc glances at the young couple. Silence. Gertrude watches them while attending to her tapestry. She looks from Marc to the two young people. Silence. Marc turns his gaze to the fire.

PATRICE *(in a reproachful but amused tone):* Natalie!

Natalie bursts out laughing. Marc looks at them again. Gertrude stands up; she assumes a detached but cheerful expression.

GERTRUDE: How wonderful to be young!

Marc starts. Silence. Amédée, embarrassed, lowers his newspaper and coughs. Achille stops his cruel game with the cat.

GERTRUDE *(very much at ease):* Look at them, Marc . . . the old castle is coming to life again . . . I'm so pleased!

Marc looks at Gertrude and then turns his head toward Natalie and Patrice. Natalie, embarrassed, has stopped playing. Patrice attaches no importance to Gertrude's remarks.

PATRICE *(laughing):* Natalie! It's your turn to play!

She turns away and gets up.

NATALIE: I can't see straight anymore . . .

PATRICE: Do you give up?

NATALIE: I'm going up to my room. I can't keep my eyes open any longer.

PATRICE: Let me show you up.

MARC: No, no, Patrice.

Patrice and Natalie stop short. Marc has spoken somewhat nervously.

MARC *(to Patrice):* Stay . . . Natalie doesn't need anyone.

Natalie goes toward the door.

NATALIE: Goodnight . . .

She leaves the room. Patrice sits down again in front of the chess board and distractedly moves the pieces around. Silence. Amédée lowers his paper.

AMÉDÉE: I think I shall follow Miss Natalie's example . . .

He coughs and stands up, almost regretfully.

GERTRUDE: Me too, I can hardly keep my eyes open . . . Goodnight.

She puts her wool away. Achille disappears. Patrice doesn't move.

MARC: Stay a moment. I want to talk to you. *(He walks up to Gertrude and Amédée.)* I'm going to marry Natalie.

Patrice is holding a chess piece; it slips from his hand and falls. Marc starts. As though the noise were a protest from Patrice, Marc turns to him.

MARC: I'm going to marry Natalie.

GERTRUDE: What? It's not possible. Doesn't the difference in age shock you, my dear Marc? . . .

MARC: Nothing you can say will change things, I have made up my mind.

He leaves the room. Patrice, still sitting at the table, does not move. He removes the chess pieces. Gertrude, taken aback by Marc's sudden departure, turns to Patrice.

GERTRUDE: Well, she's certainly handled things well!

AMÉDÉE *(timidly):* Gertrude!

Patrice does not react.

GERTRUDE *(to Patrice):* And . . . this person . . . is . . . a very old friend?

PATRICE: A childhood friend . . . I knew her when she was Achille's size.

GERTRUDE: Amédée, let's go.

They leave the room. Patrice knocks over all the chess pieces.

The courtyard.

It is the wedding day. All the local people, farmers, laborers, etc. are assembled in the courtyard, dressed in their Sunday best. The choir walks past to the sound of a march.

Natalie's room.

Marc and Natalie are standing by the window. Natalie, her arms full of flowers, is smiling at the crowd. Marc waves at them for the last time. Still waving, he speaks to Natalie, without looking at her.

MARC: You don't regret anything?

NATALIE: What is there to regret, Marc? For me it is just unbelievable . . . let me get used to it.

MARC: To me?

NATALIE: To you, to the castle, to this entire way of life, which is completely new to me.

The Frossins' apartment.

Gertrude enters first, wearing a very gaudy dress. Amédée follows her. Achille brings up the rear. All three of them look grim. Gertrude lowers herself into an armchair. The sound of the fanfare can be heard.

GERTRUDE: Alone at last! What a farce!

Amédée sits down at the table. Achille chews his gloves.

GERTRUDE *(to Achille):* Stop eating your gloves. Take them off. Go and close the window. *(Achille goes toward the window, dragging his feet.)* Well, all that remains for us to do is gather up our bits and pieces and go.

AMÉDÉE: Where to?

GERTRUDE: Do you think I know? But we are no longer welcome here, and they'll soon make us realize it.

AMÉDÉE *(sinking back in his chair):* Well, I'd put up a fight . . .

GERTRUDE *(scornfully):* That's just like you. What you call putting up a fight is just digging yourself in . . . and accepting all the insults . . . it's a disaster. Achille, come here. *(Achille has just closed the window. He goes to his mother.)* Do you like your new aunt? *(Achille shrugs his shoulders.)* Of course. Well, my little one, you must keep your eyes open. When I fight, I really fight. Patrice is in love with that girl, and he marries her off to his uncle. It's disgraceful. We must keep smiling, Amédée. And Achille will watch over the couple . . . Achille, are you listening to me?

ACHILLE: Yes, mommy.

GERTRUDE *(to Achille):* Try to catch them. We'll open poor Marc's eyes and then it'll all come out.

AMÉDÉE: Why get Achille involved in this?

GERTRUDE: You fight your way, dear, and I'll fight my way.

A tearoom. In town.

The proprietress greets and serves the few customers herself. She is wearing a wig and a black velvet ribbon around her neck. Marc, standing by the window, pushes back the curtain to look at the sky. Lightning and thunder. The rain beats down on the window. Marc joins Gertrude and Amédée, who are seated at a table. They are the only customers.

MARC: It would be better if you waited for me here.

He takes his raincoat.

GERTRUDE: When will you be back?

MARC: Oh, in three quarters of an hour, or an hour . . .

AMÉDÉE: What a delightful evening!

GERTRUDE: I shan't leave the room till the storm is over. *(lightning and thunder)* Oh! . . . and that poor child is all alone in the house!

MARC: He is not alone, Natalie's there.

GERTRUDE: Poor darling! He must be dying of fear, just like me . . . I know he won't leave his room . . .

MARC: I doubt it.

GERTRUDE: What do you mean by that?

MARC: I mean that he's got the whole house to play in.

Marc leaves.

AMÉDÉE: Charming, the way he said "to play in."

Inside the castle.

Storm. Rain against the window panes. Lightning. A gust of wind. An unfastened corridor window suddenly blows open. The wind rushes in. The curtain, normally attached to the wall by a loop, flies open, revealing Achille crouched behind it. Thunder and wind. Achille runs down the corridor. He goes down the stairs, four at a time. He is terrified by the storm. He reaches the hall as the door opens.

ACHILLE: Ah!

Patrice enters. He is soaking wet. He quickly closes the door behind him. Achille disappears. Natalie is standing in the door of the drawing room.

NATALIE: Ah! There you are.

Patrice goes up to her and takes off his jacket.

PATRICE: The family picked a good moment to go to town.

Patrice enters the drawing room, followed by Natalie. They go over to the fireplace, where a wood fire is burning. Patrice walks up and down, shaking the rain off his hands.

NATALIE: Put another log on the fire.

He picks up a log and stops in front of the fireplace.

NATALIE *(ironically):* Don't you know how?

Patrice, kneeling in front of the fire, turns toward Natalie.

PATRICE: Natalie, you don't like me.

NATALIE: What do you mean, I don't like you?

Patrice is looking at the fire, Natalie is looking straight ahead of her.

PATRICE: No, you don't like me.

NATALIE *(after a pause):* I love your uncle, Patrice.

Patrice is warming his hands.

PATRICE: Of course you do, that's not the same thing. You're always on the defensive with me.

NATALIE *(laughing):* Me?

PATRICE: Yes, you. *(pause)* Natalie ... you're sad, you're not happy ...

NATALIE: I have a sad nature; I am happy.

PATRICE: I'd like to see you gay . . . I'd like to see you do silly things.

NATALIE: Do you do silly things?

PATRICE: Do you think I wouldn't? If you insist, I'm ready to do so right now.

NATALIE: But I do insist . . . go ahead. I'll get settled.

She slides down onto the bearskin rug in front of the fire. Patrice kneels down beside her.

PATRICE: What do you say to drinking an enormous amount of whisky?

NATALIE: You want to see me high?

PATRICE: I want to see you gay.

NATALIE: Drink, if you feel like it, but I won't drink.

PATRICE: I'll mix you a magic concoction . . .

He gets up and leaves the room.

The wine cellar.

Patrice goes down several steep stairs to an unlit door. Sound of keys turning. He pushes the door. Light enters through only two air vents. Every now and then flashes of lightning illuminate the darkness. Thunder. The cellar is quite big, full of wine racks set out in zig-zag. Patrice goes down the stairs, leaving the door open behind him. As he moves forward he bumps into something. Patrice suddenly chases after someone running between the racks. He pounces upon him, and brings him out: it is Achille.

PATRICE: I've got you!

He holds Achille by the collar of his jacket.

ACHILLE *(screaming):* Let me go, you're hurting me!

Patrice puts him down on one of the racks. Achille is holding a bottle of brandy.

PATRICE: You were stealing brandy! Did you get in through the air vent? *(Achille lets go of the bottle, which smashes on the floor.)* You're drunk, you little pig!

ACHILLE: I haven't drunk anything. Let me go!

PATRICE: Well, I've got better things to do than watch over you . . . go on . . . get the hell out of here!

He puts him down on the ground and kicks him on the backside. Achille runs off screaming, climbs up the stairs, and disappears. The thunder is still rumbling.

The drawing room.

Patrice comes back into the drawing room holding several bottles.

PATRICE: Here's enough to do a thousand silly things!

NATALIE: Go on, go on, I'm full of admiration.

PATRICE: Quite right too . . .

He disappears into the dining room. Natalie smiles, stretches out on her back, and looks at the ceiling. Lightning and thunder.

PATRICE: Aren't you getting bored with me?

NATALIE: Not in the slightest.

Patrice is standing by the bar in the dining room, shaking a cocktail mixer.

PATRICE: Thank you.

He puts down the mixer and, standing in the doorway, imitates the song of the nightingale. Natalie, surprised, listens carefully. Hidden

behind the bar, Achille pours Anne's herbal wine into the mixer. Natalie sits up to look at Patrice.

NATALIE: You are a man of many talents.

PATRICE: Yes, many.

Patrice returns to the bar. He pours out the contents of the mixer and brings back two full glasses into the drawing room. The thunder rumbles softly. Achille's face appears behind the bar. His expression is no longer one of fear, but of hatred.

NATALIE *(pushing away the glass):* Not for me.

PATRICE *(sitting down beside her):* Taste it, it's not strong.

NATALIE: I hate whisky.

PATRICE: And silly things, how do you feel about them? *(He puts the glass in her hand.)* At the same time as me and all in one gulp. *(He raises his glass.)* To your happiness! *(He drinks it straight down.)*

NATALIE: You're impossible.

She drinks hers straight down. Thunder.

PATRICE: Hurrah! She drank it.

NATALIE: I didn't want to appear foolish. *(She lies down.)* And when you're drunk, what good will it do you?

He lies down next to her.

PATRICE: None at all . . . that's what's so marvelous. *(Natalie closes her eyes.)* The ceiling is dancing . . . do you see?

Natalie opens her eyes and looks at the flames dancing on the ceiling.

NATALIE: It's the fire dancing.

Silence. They speak in low voices, their heads turned toward the ceiling.

PATRICE: It's the ceiling . . .

NATALIE: It's the fire . . .

PATRICE: It's the ceiling . . .

Natalie sits up and passes her hand over her eyes.

NATALIE: What is it?

PATRICE: You've been drinking, and so have I . . . we really should drink more often . . . it's wonderful.

NATALIE: No, Patrice, no. It isn't wonderful, yet at the same time it is wonderful.

PATRICE: You can see I really am capable of doing silly things.

NATALIE: Patrice . . . I'm afraid.

Thunder. Natalie gets up onto her knees.

PATRICE: Are you afraid of the storm?

NATALIE: No, not of the storm, but I'm afraid . . . *(lightning)* Be quiet for a moment . . . *(a crash of thunder)* That time the lightning must have struck the house.

Patrice gets up onto his knees. They are both kneeling, facing each other. Patrice unconsciously moves closer to her.

PATRICE: When I was little there was a picture of Franklin that I just loved. He was chasing the lightning out of his room with a whip as though it were a dog. So if it comes in here, I'll chase it out, I won't let it come near you. *(They are looking into each other's eyes.)* **Natalie** ... *(Their faces are very close to each other.)*

NATALIE *(as though she had just discovered him):* **It's you! ... It's you! ...**

They separate. Achille is a few yards away. He had entered the room without being seen. He laughs and throws something at them before running away. It is the flask of herbal wine, labeled "Poison." It is empty. Natalie picks it up.

NATALIE *(looking at the flask and talking to herself):* **Well, we've had a narrow escape.**

PATRICE: **What is it?**

NATALIE: **Nothing ... but we've had a narrow escape.**

GERTRUDE *(in the distance):* **My goodness, how dark it is!**

Natalie does not start, as one might expect her to. She gets up. A light goes on in the hall.

GERTRUDE *(in the distance):* **Is there no one there? Where are they all?**

AMÉDÉE *(in the distance):* **Just like the storm we had two years ago. I'm soaking wet.**

Natalie goes toward the hall. Patrice remains in front of the fire. Gertrude and Amédée enter the room and shake themselves off.

GERTRUDE: **Take off your coat. You'll catch cold, and I'm the one who will have to look after you.**

Natalie walks past as though she had not seen them. Marc enters the room.

GERTRUDE *(to Natalie):* **Where's Achille?**

Natalie stops on the stairs and answers rather vaguely.

NATALIE: **I don't know.**

She continues to climb up the stairs. Marc notices that his wife is ill at ease. Gertrude senses that there is some mystery in the air and does not hesitate to increase the atmosphere of discomfort. Marc throws a worried look at the drawing room and moves toward the door. He sees Patrice sitting in front of the fire.

MARC: What are you doing?

PATRICE *(hardly moving):* Me? . . . I'm drying myself in front of the fire.

GERTRUDE *(as though she were talking about someone whose health was worrying her):* If I were you, Marc, I'd keep an eye on Patrice . . .

Patrice's room. Night.

Patrice is in bed but is not sleeping. He is staring in front of him. Footsteps can be heard outside. Moulouk, who is lying at the foot of the bed, pricks up his ears. Patrice props himself up on his elbow. The door opens slowly. Natalie's white silhouette is framed in the doorway.

PATRICE: It's you?

Natalie enters the room like a sleepwalker, closes the door, and goes toward the bed. She stops at the foot without answering. She is very pale. Natalie and Patrice talk in low voices. They are embarrassed as though face-to-face after making some confession.

PATRICE: You scared me . . . are you ill?

NATALIE: Yes, Patrice, I'm ill.

PATRICE: What's wrong with you?

NATALIE: You should never have made me drink . . .

PATRICE: A few drops of alcohol couldn't have made you ill!

NATALIE: It wasn't only alcohol.

She sits down on the edge of the bed.

PATRICE: If it were poison, I too would be ill.

NATALIE: Patrice, it's something quite ridiculous. I refuse to believe in it but it frightens me.

PATRICE: What is it?

NATALIE: Achille made us drink a mysterious herbal wine that poor Anne concocted for me . . . she was afraid that I would marry without love . . .

PATRICE: And you believe in these old women's potions?

NATALIE: Don't you believe in them Patrice?

PATRICE: Good gracious, no! It takes more than that to be poisoned. *(He takes her hand.)*

NATALIE: I wonder . . . I don't know . . . I don't know anymore . . . I wanted to find out if I alone feel the way I do.

PATRICE: Are you reassured now?

NATALIE *(after a pause):* Yes, Patrice, I'm reassured . . . *(She withdraws her hands and stands up.)* completely reassured.

PATRICE: Go back to your room. If Marc found you here, what would he think?

Natalie leaves the room the same way as she entered, like a sleepwalker.

Natalie's room.

Natalie enters her room, which is lit by a lamp on the table. She is still walking like a sleepwalker. Marc is sitting on the bed. He is fully clothed. Natalie does not see him.

MARC: Where have you been?

Natalie starts and stops walking.

NATALIE: Oh! . . . you scared me.

MARC: Why?

NATALIE: I couldn't sleep. I was walking along the corridors.

Marc watches her. She goes to the head of the bed, on the opposite side from him.

MARC *(turning toward her):* You see, I think you're somewhat nervous . . . and I think Patrice is somewhat nervous as well. *(without looking at her)* I shall probably have to ask Patrice to leave . . . *(Natalie gets into bed. Marc continues talking without looking at her.)* Natalie, people mustn't be allowed to say ugly things, they mustn't start gossiping. Gertrude is terrifying. *(He looks at her and stands up.)* You go to sleep and we won't talk about it anymore tomorrow. *(He moves nearer to her and leans over her.)* Things will take care of themselves.

NATALIE: I'm sure you're right, Marc.

MARC: Sleep well, my darling.

He kisses her on the forehead. Natalie closes her eyes. Marc turns out the light.

NATALIE: Goodnight, Marc.

Patrice's room.

Marc walks past, looking thoughtful. He reaches Patrice's room, hesitates for a moment, then goes to the door. He opens it and stops. The room is lit by a bedside lamp. The bed is empty. Somewhat surprised, he pushes open the door. He steps forward unnoticed and finds Patrice sitting on the window sill smoking a cigarette. He is wearing a bathrobe. Frogs are croaking outside.

MARC *(walking toward Patrice):* Couldn't you sleep?

PATRICE: I was smoking . . .

MARC *(stopping beside Patrice)* But you never smoke.

PATRICE: But, Uncle . . .

Marc puts his hand on his shoulder.

MARC: Listen, Patrice, I don't want people to find any reason to attack or suspect you. I'm not asking you for any explanation; you don't have to defend yourself . . . I don't believe any of the things they're saying, but they're all very unpleasant . . . I don't want Natalie's reputation ruined. She is very young . . .

PATRICE *(without looking at him):* Yes, Uncle.

MARC: You used to vanish for weeks on end; you went riding or camping; you went hunting. Leave, just as you used to do, and don't say good-bye to anyone.

PATRICE: Certainly, Uncle.

MARC *(moving away):* Let me say it once and for all. I don't want there to be any grounds for nasty gossip, I really don't.

Marc leaves the room.

The Frossins' apartment.

Achille is asleep in a quasi-loft that serves as his room. Sound of a nightingale. Achille opens his eyes, listens, and gets out of bed. He is wearing pajamas. He goes to the open skylight, climbs up onto a stool, and leans out. The nightingale is still singing.

Natalie's room.

Natalie has also heard the sound of the nightingale. She gets up and goes to the open window.

NATALIE *(in a low voice):* Is that you?

PATRICE: Yes, it's me. Listen. Come at midnight to the spring by the grotto . . . Do you hear me? It's very important.

NATALIE *(in a low voice):* I'll be there.

PATRICE *(in a low voice):* Go back . . . It's as clear as daylight out here.

Achille is seen for a moment at his skylight.

The grotto.

Clouds are scudding across the moon. At the foot of the castle is a small pond, with a humpbacked bridge. Frogs are croaking. The moon emerges from the clouds, revealing Patrice sitting at the water's edge. He is smoking a cigarette and throwing stones into the water as he waits. The frogs become silent. The surface of the water is troubled. When it settles down again, the reflection of Marc's face can be seen in the moonlight. He is leaning on a rock that overlooks the pond. Patrice sees the reflection in the water and is aghast. He does not dare move or look up. He turns his head toward the rock and starts. He has just seen Natalie's graceful silhouette come through a small, low door and follow a curving path that leads to the grotto. The frogs have started croaking again. Patrice stands up, betraying no agitation. He walks as calmly as possible to the little wooden bridge, which Natalie is just reaching. Before she sets foot on it, Patrice stops her.

PATRICE *(in a low voice):* Natalie! Don't come any further.

Taken aback, she stops. As he talks Patrice moves back to the shadow of the rock.

PATRICE *(in a loud voice, so that Marc can hear him):* It was absurd of me to ask you to come out here. *(As soon as he is hidden in the shadows and certain of not being seen by Marc, he moves his cigarette back and forth, to signal to Natalie, talking all the while.)* The Frossins are trying to dishonor us both in Marc's eyes. He wants to send me away from the castle.

Natalie is astounded. Then she begins to realize from his tone of voice and from the signs he is making that something unexpected is going on. Instinctively she looks around, without moving her head.

PATRICE: You must defend me, I beg of you. Marc will believe you. You must make him see the truth. *(Patrice is still waving his cigarette back and forth in the shadows to deny what he is saying.)* Oh! I know you don't like me very much, but still, you came here . . . so please help me.

He throws his cigarette into the water, right where Marc's face is reflected. Natalie follows the glowing trail of the cigarette and sees Marc's reflection in the water.

NATALIE: You must have faith in Marc . . . he'll understand that they're being slanderous . . . but don't ask me to come out anymore . . . it's pointless . . . what we have to say to each other can be said in front of everybody . . . goodnight!

Natalie returns quickly to the castle.

A corridor.

Marc comes up the stairs from the garden. Just as he starts down the corridor, Achille, in pajamas, comes out of the Frossin's apartment and calls him.

ACHILLE *(in a low voice):* Uncle Marc . . . *(Marc stops and turns around with a cheerful expression.)* Did you see them? *(Marc approaches Achille, who retreats instinctively.)*

MARC: I shall never forgive you . . .

Achille rushes back to his room.

The Frossin apartment.

The Frossins are playing cards.

GERTRUDE: Where are they today?

ACHILLE *(dealing the cards):* They're having a picnic on the grass.

AMÉDÉE *(raising his eyes):* On the grass!

GERTRUDE: This affair has been going on for two weeks and Marc just puts up with it. It's disgraceful.

ACHILLE: Your turn, mommy. *(She plays.)*

AMÉDÉE: Well, what do you expect? . . . They're careful when he's around. *(He plays.)*

GERTRUDE: We must find a way of drawing Marc's attention to it. *(Achille plays and picks up the cards.)*

ACHILLE *(importantly):* I have a way.

Gertrude and Amédée stop playing and turn to him.

GERTRUDE: A way?

The courtyard.

Patrice's car curves its way up to the castle. Patrice and Natalie can be heard laughing. The car comes around the corner and stops suddenly in front of Marc's car, which is parked by the step. Natalie and Patrice are thrown forward by the sudden halt. They fall back against the seat in fits of laughter. Marc comes out of the castle in traveling clothes and gets ready to leave.

MARC: You seem very merry. *(Patrice leaps out.)*

PATRICE: Natalie maintains that I don't know how to drive. *(He helps her out.)*

NATALIE *(laughing):* He's a public menace. *(They laugh.)*

MARC: I was going to leave without seeing you. I'll be back in three days. I'll send a telegram.

Patrice and Natalie are still in very high spirits. They laugh again.

Claude comes up behind Marc.

CLAUDE: Mrs. Frossin says good-bye, Sir.

They all look up and see Gertrude waving a handkerchief from her window. Gertrude's gesture sets off another fit of laughter from Patrice and Natalie, who rush off toward the house. Marc watches them with a set smile. He looks up briefly at Gertrude and waves good-bye. The car drives away.

The entrance to the tower.

A shadow passes by at the foot of the moonlit tower. The door opens and the shadow moves across to the circular stone staircase. It is Patrice, whose face is illuminated by a moonbeam shining through a skylight. He starts up the stairs as if drawn by some magnet. He climbs higher and higher as though he were scaling the sky.

Natalie's room.

Natalie is asleep, only half-covered by the sheets. Her head is thrown back to one side. Her hands are clenched on her nightgown.

The tower.

Patrice is still climbing, his face bathed in moonlight.

Natalie's room.

Patrice's footsteps are heard on the staircase. Natalie opens her eyes wide, as though she had heard these footsteps in her dreams. She sits up. Patrice appears at the top of the stairs. Natalie props herself up on her elbow.

NATALIE: Is that you?

PATRICE: Yes, it's me, Natalie.

Patrice kneels down next to her.

NATALIE: You're mad, Patrice.

PATRICE *(turning his face toward her):* Yes, I'm mad . . . I'm mad and I'm beginning to think you were right: we are poisoned. But it's a beautiful poison, Natalie.

Natalie looks at Patrice with intense passion and takes his face in her hands.

NATALIE: Patrice . . .

PATRICE *(moving to her):* We are poisoned and it's wonderful, and there's nothing we can do about it.

Natalie leans back against the pillow, pulling Patrice down with her.

NATALIE *(in a low voice):* Patrice . . .

PATRICE *(in a low voice):* . . . Nothing we can do . . .

Their cheeks touch. He turns around and kisses her. She gently breaks away from him.

NATALIE *(in a low voice):* You can't stay in this room.

PATRICE *(in a low voice):* And suppose I did stay?

Patrice suddenly leaps up. Natalie sits up. Blinded by the light, Patrice turns toward the staircase in an attempt to escape but Achille emerges from it, like an animal from its hole. Patrice turns toward the door that leads into the corridor. Gertrude is standing there. She lights another lamp. Patrice and Natalie are surrounded. Marc's door opens on the landing above. Patrice and Natalie turn around. Marc appears, lights another lamp, and, without looking at them, walks over to the bed.

MARC: It so happens that one can leave by car but return on foot. It so happens that one is not always the cleverest. Please leave us, Gertrude.

Gertrude takes Achille's hand and leaves, with a triumphant smile.

PATRICE: Uncle, in no way is this Natalie's fault . . .

MARC: I don't want any explanation. Go back to your room. I will tell you what I have decided tomorrow morning.

Patrice hesitates for a moment but gives in to Marc's authority and leaves the room. Marc goes out just as he came in, without looking at Natalie. Natalie, who is pale and drawn, has not moved. Tears roll down her cheeks.

Marc's study. The following day.

Marc is standing by the window with his back to Patrice and Natalie, who are waiting for his verdict. Having made up his mind, he suddenly turns toward them.

MARC: First of all, I don't want any explanations or tearful scenes. Patrice, I've decided that you shall leave the estate . . . *(Patrice lowers his head.)* I shan't pursue you. I shall just avoid meeting you in the future. I have given my orders. You will leave today. *(Then he turns to Natalie.)* You . . . . *(Patrice takes a step toward his uncle.)*

PATRICE: Uncle Marc . . . It's essential that . . .

MARC: I would be most grateful if you did not interrupt me . . . *(He turns back to Natalie.)* You . . . *(without looking at her)* will go back to your island, to the house where Patrice found you.

NATALIE: Marc!

MARC: Gertrude will take you in her car. I couldn't ask for a more watchful guard. You will leave today.

NATALIE: Not to the island, Marc. There's a drunkard there who will kill me. You can't do that.

MARC: I'm sure you will settle the matter, you seem to have a way with men . . . I have decided that . . . that you will go back to your island. Any discussion will be painful and will lead nowhere. *(He turns to Patrice.)* You are free to go, Patrice. I shall keep Natalie in her room until her departure. *(He turns his back on him.)*

PATRICE: Good-bye, Marc!

A road.

Gertrude is driving her convertible along a sunny road in the deserted country. Achille is sitting next to her. Natalie is alone in the back seat. The engine keeps missing. It's smoking.

GERTRUDE: This car is going to explode — what can be wrong with it?

ACHILLE: It's smoking.

GERTRUDE: I can see it's smoking!

The car slows down, splutters, moves off again in fits and starts, and finally comes to a complete halt.

GERTRUDE: It's broken down. That's fine, in this heat.

ACHILLE: We'll have to wait for a car to stop. *(He stands up on the seat and looks at the horizon.)*

GERTRUDE: I should have taken the main road. Put your hanky over your head.

ACHILLE: Mommy, a car! . . .

GERTRUDE: We're saved!

She turns around and takes a look. Achille is pointing: a car is coming toward them at high speed. Achille waves at it, still standing on the seat. Gertrude takes out her handkerchief and signals with it.

GERTRUDE *(shouting):* Mister, mister! . . .

But Achille, who can see better than she can, quiets down. He has recognized the car.

ACHILLE: Mommy, it's Patrice.

GERTRUDE *(taken aback):* What?

Upon hearing Patrice's name, Natalie turns around quickly. And indeed, Patrice comes up in his Ford and parks next to the broken-down car. Moulouk is with Patrice.

PATRICE: Have you broken down?

GERTRUDE: Perhaps you can tell me what you're doing on this road.

PATRICE: Yes, Aunt: I'm the knight in shining armor. I see I've arrived at the right moment.

He jumps into Gertrude's car, next to Natalie.

GERTRUDE: You try and get along with my car and we'll take yours.

Patrice leans forward between Achille and Gertrude.

PATRICE: That would be a terrible mistake.

He taps Gertrude on the shoulder.

GERTRUDE *(shouting):* Don't touch me!

PATRICE: What are you shouting for? I don't wish you any harm, and Achille is a big strong man who realizes that it is in his own interest to keep quiet.

Patrice jumps into his car.

GERTRUDE *(starting to get out):* He's mad.

PATRICE: Stay where you are.

GERTRUDE: Are you trying to order me around? Don't forget I'm representing your uncle here.

PATRICE: And no one could represent him worse than you.

Patrice takes Natalie's hand and helps her across the seats from one car to the other.

GERTRUDE: You conspired this together; you'll pay for it.

Patrice settles down at the steering wheel of his car.

PATRICE: There's no conspiracy. I caused your breakdown. I cut the fan belt.

GERTRUDE: It's incredible.

Patrice, who had left his engine running, sets off.

GERTRUDE *(shouting):* Achille . . . run! Get down, no . . . don't . . . Murderer, murderer, hooligan! . . .

The Ford disappears along the road into the beautiful countryside.

A hut in the snow.

Morning. A very poor hut, with no comforts whatsoever. The broken panes are replaced with sheets of newspaper. It is a hideout for poachers. Inside, there is a stove, a table, and two chairs.

Moulouk goes to a corner of the hut where there is a low, makeshift bed. Only Patrice's and Natalie's hair can be seen, and Patrice's hand, which is hanging down. Moulouk licks his hand . . . Patrice wakes up. He sits up, smiles at Moulouk, and strokes him. He is wearing a heavy, turtleneck sweater. There are no sheets on the bed. They are sleeping fully clothed, as though camping. Patrice turns toward Natalie. She is pale and drawn. Her expression as she sleeps is serious. Patrice imitates the nightingale's song. She wakes up. She is wearing Patrice's clothes. She looks at him and tries to smile.

PATRICE: How do you feel this morning?

NATALIE: Fine, Patrice.

PATRICE *(leaning over and kissing her):* You were sleeping without me, like a little girl. Were you dreaming?

NATALIE: Since we ran away, I've been dreaming of all this, and when I'm awake, I think I'm still dreaming . . .

PATRICE: I don't like the people in your dreams. I don't know them and they don't know me.

NATALIE: Oh, but the people in my dreams know you . . .

Natalie strokes his face. Her hand is very cold.

PATRICE: You're frozen.

NATALIE: Yes, I am a little cold.

PATRICE: I'll make a fire.

He gets up and goes outside. Sound of an axe cutting wood. Moulouk comes into the hut. He is carrying something in his mouth. Natalie turns around and looks at the dog. Her expression changes. Moulouk sits down beside her and seems to be offering her the object he had picked up: a fur glove, still full of snow. Natalie turns it over and over in her hand.

PATRICE: Moulouk, shut the door... *(Natalie hides the glove behind her. Patrice is laden down with logs for the fire. He walks over to the stove.)* A walking forest!

He sets to work at the stove.

NATALIE: I'm causing you a lot of trouble.

PATRICE: Oh, terrible trouble!

NATALIE: Patrice, what are we going to do?

PATRICE: Make a fire.

Natalie looks up at the dancing shadows of the flames.

NATALIE: I've got you involved in such a terrible affair...

PATRICE: Well, because I've been promised work in town, I'll find a place where we can hide ... where I can look after you.

NATALIE: Patrice ... I'm afraid of falling ill and showing you a side of me that'll frighten you ... that you won't like ...

Patrice comes up to her, kneels, and takes her in his arms.

PATRICE: You must be feeling far worse than you'll admit ... *(He puts his hand on her forehead.)* You have a fever ... It's all my fault.

NATALIE: It's our fault. It was madness ...

PATRICE: Yes, my love. But such beautiful madness. And I would no longer want to live without this madness.

NATALIE *(with a feeling of great love):* Patrice ...

PATRICE *(holding her tighter):* I'm horribly selfish. I'm going into town right away. I'll be back this evening.

He kisses her and stands up. She wants to cry out.

NATALIE: Patrice!

Patrice puts on his jacket, turns around, and looks at her tenderly.

PATRICE: I hate to leave you all alone.

She is sitting up and looking at him despairingly.

NATALIE *(her voice almost failing):* I won't be alone ... I'll keep Moulouk.

Patrice talks to Moulouk, who is hovering around him.

PATRICE: Moulouk will watch over you. Moulouk, come here. *(He kneels down, takes hold of the dog's head, and talks in his ear.)* I entrust you with my love.

As though he had understood, Moulouk stays behind in the hut. Patrice leaves.

In front of the hut.

Natalie calls Patrice from inside the hut. Patrice turns around and runs back. Natalie is standing motionless in the door of the hut. She clings to him and kisses him as though it were for the last time.

PATRICE: I keep leaving and coming back.

Natalie watches him go. He gives a final wave and disappears. Suddenly she starts. She looks over her shoulder.

NATALIE: I was expecting you ... *(It is Marc, carrying a fur coat over his arm.)* I knew you had been here ... I knew you'd come back.

She goes back into the hut, leaving the door open behind her. Marc stays outside, leaning against the wall in the doorway.

MARC: Last night I came here with murderous intentions . . . I saw you sleeping and I was forced to relent. *(a pause)* It would be best if you agreed to come with me.

NATALIE *(coming to the door):* Take me away as quickly as possible.

Marc puts the fur coat over her shoulders.

MARC: Take whatever you want to bring with you . . .

NATALIE: I have nothing, Marc . . . I came with nothing.

She turns around and gazes at the hut.

MARC *(following her look):* Do you regret leaving this hut?

She does not answer him but goes back to the door of the hut. She leans her head against it, closes her eyes, and strokes the wall. She stays there, with her cheek against the door until Marc takes her by the shoulders and pulls her gently away. She opens her eyes, unable to drag herself away from the door.

NATALIE: Take me away . . . quickly . . . quickly . . . as quickly as possible . . .

Marc pulls her away and helps her walk. Moulouk hesitates for a moment, looks behind him, and follows them through the snow.

In front of the hut. Evening. Sunset.

The chimney is no longer smoking. There is no light inside the hut. A heavy silence. Patrice, carrying parcels under his arm, whistles the nightingale's song. He stops, listens . . . Nothing moves . . . He starts again . . . stops . . . listens. Silence. He is worried. He walks up to the hut and calls . . .

PATRICE: Natalie! . . . Natalie . . . *(Across the beautiful countryside, lit up by the setting sun, one can hear Patrice's voice, becoming more and more anguished, howling inside the hut.)* Natalie! Natalie! Natalie!

A little town perched on a hill. Patrice stops his car in front of a garage. He honks his horn without getting out of the car. A mechanic comes out of the garage and goes up to him.

Patrice is dusty and badly shaven. One can tell that he has driven for miles. Nothing more can affect him now.

THE MECHANIC: Gas?

PATRICE: No.

The mechanic sees the flat tire.

THE MECHANIC: You want that repaired?

PATRICE: No . . . I want to sell my car. You wouldn't know anyone interested in antiques?

The mechanic purses his lips and looks at the car.

THE MECHANIC: Better speak to the boss.

Patrice drives the car into the garage. Ukelele music can be heard.
The car stops in front of a small office. It is a jumble of papers,
pamphlets, spare parts, cups, sporting trophies, a head of a woman
in plaster of Paris with a moustache penciled on it, etc. The owner,
Lionel, is sitting with his feet up on the table, humming away and
playing the ukelele.

PATRICE *(in the doorway):* I hope I'm not disturbing you.

Lionel stops playing and turns toward the door.

LIONEL: Patrice.

He gets up. They shake hands.

PATRICE: So you own a garage, do you?

LIONEL: Why shouldn't I own a garage?

PATRICE: I just didn't imagine you as a garage owner.

LIONEL: There are happy men who own cars and unhappy men who own garages. There you are.

Patrice turns around and nods toward his car.

PATRICE: Have you seen my car?

Lionel hoists himself up and takes a look.

LIONEL: Well, I would say she's come of age. Do you want to buy another one?

Patrice walks around the office. It is obvious he does not really care if his car is sold or not.

PATRICE: Not exactly. I want to sell this one because I have no money. I have fallen out with my uncle. He threw me out of the house.

LIONEL: Because of his troupe of dwarfs?

PATRICE: That's got something to do with it.

LIONEL: Congratulations. Yet another abandoned child. Just our kind.

PATRICE: Whose kind?

LIONEL: My sister and myself. We are abandoned children. Mother is in Morocco . . . she went to join father, who was posted there.

She insisted that I have a job, which explains the garage. And that's that. Father and mother have never taken any notice whatsoever of us since. So we're an old couple, brother and sister. Where are you living?

PATRICE: Nowhere. I've just arrived.

LIONEL: Well then, you must stay with us.

PATRICE: No, no, I'll take a room in a hotel and I'll sell my car.

Lionel advances threateningly on him.

LIONEL: And what about the "Good Works for the Upkeep of Abandoned Children?"

He brings out a revolver which he points at Patrice. He shoots, and a cigarette pops out of it.

LIONEL: You are poor. I am rich. I own a garage. And I shall buy your car. I am a god.

Patrice, won over, takes the cigarette. Lionel goes over to a small door and knocks.

NATALIE II *(behind the door):* Who is it?

LIONEL: The police.

NATALIE II: Idiot!

LIONEL *(to Patrice):* That's what it's like in this house.

He opens the door and shows Patrice into a tiny, cluttered room. It appears to be a girl's room and a junk room at the same time. On a sofa in a corner, Natalie II is buried in a detective novel, smoking a cigarette. The room is very smoky. The shutters are closed to keep out the sun. Natalie II is reading by lamplight. She is dark-haired.

LIONEL: Let me introduce you to an "abandoned child." No money. Car for sale.

Patrice nods his head.

LIONEL *(to Natalie II):* He will stay in mother's room. *(to Patrice)* This is my sister, Natalie.

When he hears the name "Natalie," Patrice starts. He looks at Lionel and his sister. Natalie II observes him without the slightest embarrassment, showing only indifference and superiority. Lionel beckons to Patrice.

LIONEL: Come, I'll show you to your room.

Lionel climbs over the sofa and opens a door which looks rarely used, because the sofa is in front of it. Patrice has to climb onto the sofa to follow him. Natalie II, who had turned back to her book, throws it down. She crawls over to the end of the sofa and looks through the open door at Patrice, who is following Lionel up the stairs.

Patrice's room.

The room is furnished like a doctor's waiting room. It used to be Lionel's mother's room. Lionel enters, followed by Patrice.

LIONEL: Here's your room, old boy. In period taste, though I don't know what period. It's mother's taste.

Natalie II has followed them.

NATALIE II: We have adjoining rooms. *(They turn toward her.)* If this taste gives you nightmares you can wake me.

PATRICE: I feel terribly embarrassed.

NATALIE II: Are you that stupid? *(Patrice is surprised.)*

LIONEL: You'll get used to it.

NATALIE II *(turning around):* You seemed very taken aback by my name. Don't you like it?

PATRICE: Are you that stupid?

The brother and sister look at each other and burst out laughing.

LIONEL: He's getting used to it.

The castle. Natalie's room.

The window looks out over the grounds. Natalie is in bed. She is pale, with hollow cheeks. Marc is sitting on the edge of the bed holding her hand. Moulouk is lying on the carpet. Marc is watching over Natalie with a worried expression. Natalie turns her head and seems to come out of her lethargy.

MARC: Do you think you can sleep?

NATALIE: Yes, Marc . . .

MARC: Is there anything you want?

NATALIE: No, Marc . . . Listen . . . Yes . . . I would like to ask you something . . . *(Marc kisses her hand and looks at her questioningly. Natalie closes her eyes.)* I would like to change rooms.

MARC: Change rooms? Why?

NATALIE: I almost always have my eyes closed . . . *(She opens her eyes and looks around.)* When I open them *(with great weariness)* it's so tiring, Marc . . . I'd like to change rooms.

A short pause.

MARC: It's agreed then, Natalie. I'll instruct them to prepare the room in the north wing. It's smaller and more cheerful. You can almost see the sea. We'll get you settled tomorrow.

NATALIE: You are kind to me, Marc.

The Frossins' apartment.

Amédée is mending a rapier with a blowtorch. The rapier is held in a vise on the edge of the table.

AMÉDÉE: But what's the matter with her?

Gertrude is sitting at the table, playing solitaire.

GERTRUDE: The matter is that her darling Patrice is far away . . .

AMÉDÉE: The doctor doesn't find her at all well.

GERTRUDE: She could trick all the doctors. She's pretending to be fading away in order to soften up Marc.

Amédée switches off the blowtorch, puts it down, and speaks, measuring the effect of his words.

AMÉDÉE: Well, I have news of Patrice.

Gertrude drops her cards.

GERTRUDE: You?

AMÉDÉE: Yes, me . . . everyone thinks I'm so useless . . .

GERTRUDE: What do you know?

AMÉDÉE *(still looking at his work):* He's living in town with a garage owner and his sister, a very bad kind of girl, and he never leaves her side.

GERTRUDE: How do you know all this?

AMÉDÉE: Every now and then I go into town to buy more weapons.

GERTRUDE: For once your trophies are of some use . . . Tell me more . . .

AMÉDÉE: I don't know any more. The pretty trio is always together. It seems that Patrice might even marry the girl . . .

GERTRUDE: But that's amazing news!

She glances at Amédée's work. She puts out her hand, grasps the rapier, and snaps it in two at the place where it had just been soldered.

GERTRUDE: Surely one can have a sword soldered in a garage?

AMÉDÉE *(admiringly):* You really are astonishing!

The garage.

Patrice is jacking up the front of a car. Lionel, his head buried in the engine, looks up and watches Patrice work the jack with an absent expression.

LIONEL: Patrice, you're so gloomy! What's wrong with you.

PATRICE: Nothing's wrong with me.

LIONEL: And suppose I told you what was wrong with you? Hmm?

Patrice unscrews something inside the engine.

PATRICE: I'd be very curious to know.

LIONEL: You're in love with Natalie.

Patrice straightens up suddenly.

PATRICE: What?

LIONEL: You're in love with Natalie, and you look just like someone who believes that the woman he loves doesn't love him. *(Patrice buries himself in the engine again.)* Well, that's where you're wrong. I know my sister. She's crazy about you.

PATRICE *(stands up, laughing):* She thinks I'm a fool. A worthy fool. But a fool.

LIONEL: There are ways and means of saying it. She loves you. You can see it a mile off.

Patrice gets into the car and tries to start the engine. Lionel gets in next to him. Patrice pushes the starter again.

PATRICE: If it were true, I would leave immediately.

LIONEL: Why?

PATRICE: Why? *(He pushes the starter again.)* Because if your sister were in love with me, I wouldn't stay here another moment.

LIONEL: Oh, you're so boring!

Lionel automatically pulls out the choke as Patrice tries the starter once more. The engine starts.

PATRICE: And your father and mother, what about them?

LIONEL: Father doesn't even know if we are married or not and mother shouted to Natalie from the train, "I hope you're married by the time we get back." They're a little strange.

Lionel turns around and sees a customer.

LIONEL: A customer. Get rid of him ... I want to talk to you and clear up this matter.

A man stops in front of the office door. He is carrying a long black sheath. He turns around. It is Amédée.

AMÉDÉE *(pretending surprise):* Well now, this is a surprise!

PATRICE: Good morning.

AMÉDÉE: I wanted to ask the garage owner if he could solder a sword for me.

Patrice ushers him into the office.

PATRICE: Couldn't be simpler.

Amédée enters and pulls out the rapier from its sheath.

AMÉDÉE: Are you the owner?

PATRICE: No. He's a friend of mine.

Patrice has joined Amédée by the desk and is looking at the rapier.

AMÉDÉE: Good ... good ... good ... Well, congratulations! The great news is true, then?

PATRICE: What great news?

AMÉDÉE: That you're getting married?

PATRICE: Me? Who told you that tale?

AMÉDÉE: It was Natalie. She was so happy. She came rushing over to Gertrude to tell her.

PATRICE: Is Natalie well?

AMÉDÉE: She was a little ill. But she's as fit as a fiddle now. Almost ruddy. And putting on weight. *(Patrice puts some papers away.)* She's looking after the estate. She gets all over the place . . .

PATRICE: And it was she who spoke to you about this marriage?

AMÉDÉE: She said: "At last, Patrice is getting married. We are so relieved, Marc and I." So . . . I congratulate you . . .

LIONEL *(entering the office):* What is it?

Amédée and Patrice turn toward the door.

PATRICE: He wants this weapon soldered.

Lionel picks up the rapier from the desk.

LIONEL: This is a garage. We don't solder arms.

AMÉDÉE: But . . .

LIONEL *(handing him the rapier):* Take it away. You don't think I'm going to waste my time soldering arms, do you?

Amédée picks up the sheath.

AMÉDÉE: All right . . . all right . . . Don't lose your temper. I'll take it away. You are most ungracious.

LIONEL: I am what I am. Good day.

AMÉDÉE: Good day Patrice.

He leaves the garage.

LIONEL: Do you know him?

PATRICE: A little.

LIONEL: What a bore! *(He takes up the interrupted conversation again.)* Listen to me, Patrice. How much longer will you refuse to understand?

PATRICE: There's nothing to understand.

LIONEL: I know her better than you do, and I know you. You love her and you're dead scared that she'll laugh at you so you pretend not to believe that she loves you. *(They have returned to the car they were repairing.)* Do you find her attractive?

PATRICE: Yes, I do, Lionel. In fact I find her much too attractive . . . But love is another matter . . .

Patrice kneels down to inspect one of the front tires.

LIONEL: Goodness, you're so complicated!

He kneels down beside Patrice, who is checking the steering by moving the tire.

LIONEL: You find her attractive; you love her. So, marry her and help me run the garage. It's wonderful. To begin with, you have no family. We are your family. You're not going to go on living alone, waiting for your uncle to choose you a wife! *(Patrice stops and looks at him silently.)* What do you think?

PATRICE: Things have a way of happening. It's better to let them happen.

Patrice stands up and takes hold of the handle on the jack.

LIONEL: The most important thing is that you find her attractive. Do you find her attractive?

PATRICE: Yes, I do . . .

He works the jack. The car is lowered to the ground.

Patrice's room.

Patrice is sitting on the carpet, leaning against the bed, with his arms clasped around his legs and his head resting on his knees.

Someone knocks on the door. Patrice stirs from his lethargy, gets up, and lies down on the bed.

PATRICE: Come in.

Natalie II enters the room. She is wearing a dressing gown fastened with one of her brother's ties. Patrice turns around.

PATRICE: Ah, it's you.

NATALIE II: You're so formal for someone who's been living with me for two weeks. I find it very strange. *(She goes up to the bed.)* I'm sure you find it a little odd, a young girl coming into a boy's room at night.

PATRICE *(not moving):* You really believe I'm incredibly stupid don't you?

NATALIE II: Just a little stupid. I was bored all alone. I couldn't sleep. Do you sleep well?

PATRICE: I sleep as much as possible.

NATALIE II: I think sleeping is a waste of time. Don't you like life?

PATRICE: Life doesn't like me.

NATALIE II: That's not very nice.

PATRICE: I'm not talking about my present life.

NATALIE II: Were you unhappy at your uncle's?

PATRICE: It would be very kind of you never to mention that to me again.

NATALIE II *(standing up):* Well, I'll let you get some sleep. Give me a cigarette.

PATRICE *(handing her a pack from the table):* Have I been very rude?

NATALIE II: I'm getting used to it.

She leaves the room. Patrice stands up, looks at the door, and hesitates for a moment. Then he makes up his mind and opens Natalie II's door without knocking. Natalie II is standing in the middle of the room. She turns around. She is lighting a cigarette.

NATALIE II: You're making progress. You don't knock any more . . . well . . . come in!

She goes toward the bed and sits with her hands folded on her lap. He joins her. She switches on the radio.

NATALIE II *(without looking at him):* What is it? Do you want your cigarette back?

Patrice sits down next to her.

PATRICE: Listen, if I'm annoying you, hit me. *(The radio is playing a dance tune.)* Is it true that you love me?

Natalie II is turning the radio dial from one station to another. Static on the radio.

NATALIE II *(bluntly, without looking at him):* Yes.

PATRICE: Do you want to marry me?

Natalie II looks for another station. Static again.

NATALIE II *(as before):* Yes.

PATRICE: Natalie.

Throughout this scene, Natalie II keeps fiddling with the radio, which crackles disagreeably, without stopping for more than a second or two at any one station.

NATALIE II: And when are we going to commit this folly?

PATRICE: Very soon. We were going to take a holiday soon. Let's take it now.

NATALIE II: Why not?

PATRICE: I know of an island and a charming old lady who will put us up.

NATALIE II: Where is this island of yours?

PATRICE: It's a fisherman's island.

LIONEL *(suddenly opening the door):* Well? *(Lionel enters the room with an accordion under his arm.)* Have you decided to keep me from working all night?

Natalie II and Patrice stand up.

NATALIE II: No, but we've decided to get married.

LIONEL: You're ludicrous.

He goes between them.

NATALIE II: Yes, ludicrous. And Patrice has found a deserted island. We're going there.

Lionel puts the accordion down on the bed.

PATRICE: What do you think?

LIONEL: We'll repopulate it.

NATALIE II: A deserted island with you two . . . what fun.

Lionel leaps at Patrice, rolls him over on the bed, laughs, and bites his leg.

NATALIE II *(angrily):* Go and fight elsewhere! Get out!

Anne's house. The ground floor.

Anne, perched on a chair, is fixing a sort of star-shaped wreath of garlands onto the ceiling. Footsteps are heard coming down the stairs. Anne turns her head and stops what she is doing. It is Natalie II.

NATALIE II: Has Patrice come down?

Anne gives Natalie II a funny look.

ANNE *(mechanically):* He went out, about an hour ago.

NATALIE II *(disappointed):* Ah.

ANNE: It's funny . . . I can't see you come down those stairs without thinking of Natalie.

Natalie II stops and turns around in surprise.

NATALIE II: Of Natalie?

Anne gets down off the chair.

ANNE: I mean mine . . . the one that married Patrice's uncle.

Natalie II is taken by surprise, this is the first she has heard of another Natalie.

NATALIE II *(in a neutral voice):* Ah . . . of course . . . I'd forgotten she was called Natalie . . . *(She goes to the window, leans out, and looks at the sea.)* Didn't Patrice say where he was going?

ANNE: Perhaps your brother has seen him.

Lionel, loaded down with fishing tackle and with the accordion slung around his neck, comes down the stairs on all fours.

LIONEL *(very gaily):* Here comes the jolly fisherman! The jolly fisherman and music . . . Have you seen Patrice?

NATALIE II: No.

Lionel stops at the table and drinks a large mug of coffee that had been prepared for him.

LIONEL *(energetically):* He can join us later. I don't want to waste any time.

Anne looks at Lionel with amusement. He puts his arm around her waist. She laughs merrily.

LIONEL: There's no wedding without a feast, and no feast without music. Here's the music, now for the fish.

He kisses Anne on the cheek and goes over to his sister. He looks up at the garlands.

LIONEL: Wonderful! Are you coming Natalie?

NATALIE II: Get everything ready. I'll join you at the boat.

LIONEL: Well, hurry up then. We've got to really astound the inhabitants with this wedding!

He leaves the room.

ANNE *(to Natalie II):* Your coffee will get cold.

NATALIE II *(turning around):* Patrice often speaks to me about his

aunt and uncle. Do you know them?

She picks up the mug and drinks.

ANNE: I don't know his uncle, but I know Natalie, my Natalie.

Natalie II sips her coffee. The mug covers her face; only her eyes can be seen.

NATALIE II: I'd very much like to know her. *(She drinks.)* You wouldn't have a photo of her? *(She drinks.)*

ANNE *(mysteriously):* Would you like to see?

NATALIE II: Well, she is my aunt . . . *(She drinks.)*

ANNE *(as before):* Don't tell Patrice that I showed you . . .

NATALIE II *(drinking):* Why not?

She puts down the mug. Anne brings out a photo.

ANNE: Because he'll be angry with me. Young women are always a little jealous of each other.

NATALIE II: Young women?

Anne gives her the photo. Natalie II takes it apprehensively and looks at it. Her face falls.

ANNE: It's a photo from last year, and you can't see very well because it's taken against the sun. You should see her in the shade! Light all around her. She looks like a seagull . . .

While Anne is talking, Natalie II cannot take her eyes off the photo. When she finally looks up, she has a haunted look on her face. She runs out, clutching the photo.

ANNE: But . . . what's this? *(shouting)* Give me back the photo! Miss! Miss! *(She runs to the window and leans out.)* Give it back!

In front of the boathouse.

A rocky promontory juts out into the sea. There is a small abandoned chapel, which serves as a boathouse and workshop. Some old boats are rotting in the sun.

At the end of the promontory, Lionel is busy loading a fishing boat, which is tied to the jetty. Natalie II comes around to the side of the boathouse. Lionel, who has finished loading his tackle, climbs up cheerfully to meet his sister.

LIONEL: What about Patrice?

NATALIE II: Patrice won't be coming.

LIONEL: Did he say so?

NATALIE II: No.

Lionel is about to take the oars down to the boat. He does not attach much importance to Patrice's absence. Natalie II calls him back.

NATALIE II: Lionel!

He retraces his steps. Natalie II tries as hard as possible not to show that she is upset, but Lionel is suddenly intrigued by her expression and the tone of her voice.

NATALIE II: Patrice will never marry me.

LIONEL: Patrice? But the wedding's tomorrow.

NATALIE II *(turning her head away)*: We will never get married.

LIONEL: Why not?

NATALIE II: It's very simple. Patrice doesn't love me.

LIONEL: What are you talking about? Did he talk to you?

NATALIE II: He didn't talk to me because I haven't seen him, and I haven't seen him because, even when I do see him and talk to him, he's invisible. *(She looks at Lionel, who makes a sign meaning "You're crazy.")* No, Lionel ... I'm quite certain. *(talking to herself)* Patrice doesn't live in our world ... our laughter irritates him . . . our lightheartedness kills him . . . and when he doesn't avoid us . . . he's even further away.

LIONEL: You're crazy! Absolutely crazy! Patrice loves us. Patrice loves you. After all, he's the one that brought us to the island.

Natalie II turns toward him. She tries to hold back her tears as she speaks.

NATALIE II: It's not me he's looking for here . . . it's not my name he speaks . . . He's looking for a ghost, Lionel . . . Do you want to know the real Natalie? . . . Here she is. *(She shows him the photo of the other Natalie.)* It's his uncle's wife. I'm just the shadow of that Natalie.

Lionel takes the photo and looks at it as though the truth had just dawned on him.

LIONEL: I shall smash his face in.

NATALIE II: There's nothing we can do about it, my friend!

LIONEL *(louder):* I shall smash his face in!

NATALIE II *(trying to hold him back):* Let it drop, Lionel . . . *(He runs off, still holding the photo.)* Lionel!

He disappears.

The Velo Bar.

Patrice is the only customer. He is sitting in the very place where Natalie sat when he saw her for the first time. The owner fills two glasses and comes over to him.

THE OWNER: Yes, sir . . . Morolt is dead, and shall I tell you something? . . . Well . . . we were all sorry.

Patrice is sitting with his elbows on the table, looking into the distance.

THE OWNER: Yes indeed. What do you expect; here, they were all proud of a fellow that scared them so. *(He puts down the glasses and sits down.)* And anyway . . . you see . . . there're not many people around here . . . They came here to be scared by Morolt, that's how it was. When he fell into the water, dead-drunk he was . . . we watched him drown, nobody made a move to get him out, but, the next day . . . they were all very sad.

He drinks.

Lionel comes in, out of breath, having run all the way. He looks around, sees Patrice, and goes up to the table. The owner gets up and moves away. Lionel throws down the photo onto the table.

LIONEL: Explain.

PATRICE *(sees the photo and looks up):* Explain what? . . . since you already know.

LIONEL: I'm going to smash your face in.

PATRICE *(not moving):* Keep calm, Lionel.

Lionel makes a threatening gesture. Patrice puts his hand on his arm.

LIONEL: Why did you agree to marry my sister?

PATRICE: Because I liked living with you . . . I liked you a lot, Lionel . . . I thought it was the only way to cure myself.

LIONEL: What does this woman mean to you exactly?

Patrice does not answer. His face is expressionless. He looks straight ahead. His eyes fill with tears. One rolls down his cheek. Lionel is very upset and changes his attitude at once. He sits down.

LIONEL *(with great warmth):* Patrice!

PATRICE *(turning his head away):* Oh! Please . . .

Lionel is slumped in his chair. He does not know what to do.

LIONEL: What's going to become of us?

PATRICE: Do I disgust you?

LIONEL: No ... I would like to save Natalie and you; I'd like to save you ... Oh, I wish that ...

Lionel mechanically picks up the photo and looks at it.

PATRICE: Listen, Lionel ... listen to me ... After this, I won't ask any more of you ... *(Lionel is still holding the photo.)* Just once, one more time ... I would like to see her again, Natalie ... Yes ... to see her again ... I'd like you to see her ... Let's go to the castle ... we can hide ... If I can bear it, if it's true she's forgotten everything ... if it's true, and you see it, then I swear I'll be strong. I swear I'll marry your sister and I'll live only for her!

LIONEL *(lowering his head):* You know I'd do anything.

PATRICE: Let's set sail immediately. *(He puts his hands on Lionel's shoulders.)* You're a good man, Lionel!

LIONEL: Oh! Please ...

The boathouse.

Lionel looks around carefully, but his sister has gone. He signals to Patrice and they go over to the motorboat. They set off. The boat disappears out to sea. Natalie II, who is hiding inside the boathouse, sees them go. She does not move. She stands there watching them with a hard expression on her face.

The castle grounds.

Night has fallen. Patrice and Lionel make their way past the grotto, over the bridge toward the castle. When they reach the tower, Patrice goes forward alone, leaving Lionel hidden behind a bush. He lifts up his face toward Natalie's room, and whistles the nightingale's song in the moonlight.

Natalie's room.

The room is empty. The bed, lit up by a moonbeam, is also empty. Natalie has changed rooms.

The grounds.

Patrice stops, waits, and as nothing moves, whistles again, even louder. Moulouk comes out of his kennel, pulling at his leash, but not barking. He has recognized his master. He pricks his ears. Patrice becomes more and more worried. He whistles again. In the light of the moon, Achille's face can be seen at his skylight. He is intrigued by the nightingale song. Lionel realizes that Patrice's efforts are in vain. He goes up to him and puts his hand on his shoulder. Patrice stops whistling and looks at him with a desperate and bewildered expression.

Patrice, his face covered in tears, starts whistling again. From the corner of Achille's window, the barrel of a gun appears, lowered in their direction. Patrice stops whistling; he turns around. Moulouk has broken his leash. He runs madly toward Patrice and jumps into his arms. Patrice holds him very close.

PATRICE *(in a low voice with deep anger):* I've understood . . .

LIONEL *(putting his arm round Patrice's shoulder):* Come, Patrice . . . let's go.

Lionel pulls him away. As they walk toward the little bridge with Moulouk following, Achille aims the gun at them. The barrel shines in the moonlight. Just as Patrice reaches the uncovered part of the garden, Achille shoots. Patrice is motionless, his hands clenched on his leg. He lets out a cry of pain. Lionel rushes forward to hold him up. The barrel of the gun is withdrawn into the skylight. Lionel and Patrice are still near the little wooden bridge. Lionel ties up Patrice's leg.

LIONEL: Does it hurt?

PATRICE: It doesn't matter. Help me. We've got to get out of here at all costs.

LIONEL: Ah! The bastards!

Marc's room.

Marc has his hand on the light switch. He listens for a moment, then throws back the blankets, gets out of bed, and puts on his bathrobe.

The Frossins' apartment.

Amédée awakes and sits up with a worried look. Gertrude opens her eyes and switches on the bedside lamp.

Amédée appears in the doorway of the room, dragging his slippers behind him, sleepily trying to tie a knot in his bathrobe belt. He goes to Achille's room, just as Gertrude comes out of it, with her finger on her lips.

AMÉDÉE: Did he hear anything?

GERTRUDE: Sh! *(She points at Achille through the open door. He is pretending to be asleep.)* He's asleep.

They leave the room noiselessly.

A marsh.

Patrice and Lionel are crossing a marsh covered with bushes. Lionel is holding up Patrice, who is fighting against the pain. He drags his bloody leg behind him, often getting it covered with mud up to the knee. Moulouk splashes them with dirty water.

LIONEL: Is this really a shortcut? . . . I think we're lost.

PATRICE *(panting):* No . . . no . . . I know the way . . . it's over there . . . we'll soon be out of here . . .

Suddenly Patrice slips. His leg sinks into the mud, and he falls into the slime. Lionel helps him up. Patrice is dizzy.

LIONEL: Patrice! Patrice!

Patrice makes a superhuman effort, stands up, and walks.

PATRICE: I'll manage . . .

LIONEL: You can't go on, it's impossible.

PATRICE: No . . . no . . . I'll make it. Put my arm around your neck. I must get back to the island . . . I can hold on until then . . . Let's go . . .

They set off again.

The hall in the castle.

Marc comes up to Gertrude and Amédée, who are standing in the middle of the hall. They do not look very reassured.

MARC: I can't find anything unusual anywhere.

AMÉDÉE: And yet I'm certain I heard a shot.

GERTRUDE: And Moulouk didn't even bark . . . a fine watchdog he is!

At that moment, Amédée, who was looking all around in fear, lets out a cry.

AMÉDÉE: Ah!

The others turn toward the staircase. Natalie is standing there in a white nightgown looking like a ghost. Claude comes into the hall carrying a gun. All three turn toward the door. Gertrude starts.

CLAUDE: Nothing!

GERTRUDE: Oh! You scared me!

CLAUDE: I found nothing . . . I've been all around the castle . . .

Nothing . . . But there's one thing that surprised me . . . Moulouk has disappeared . . . he broke his leash . . .

Natalie collapses in a faint on the stairs.

At sea.

It is dawn. Patrice is stretched out in the boat. He leans against Lionel, his head thrown back, his eyes closed. He is in great pain. The waves break over his leg and wash the wound.

The boathouse.

Lionel and Jules, the owner of the boat, carry Patrice, who is unconscious, into the boathouse. It is full of all kinds of boats, nets, ropes, and other accessories. They put him down on an upturned flat-bottomed boat.

LIONEL *(to Jules):* Quickly . . . go and fetch Anne and my sister and tell Anne that he's badly wounded; tell her to bring whatever's necessary.

Jules leaves. Lionel leans over Patrice, who is slowly coming to.

LIONEL: You're badly hurt . . . don't move . . . don't talk.

PATRICE *(closing his eyes, moving his head slightly, and sighing):* Natalie . . .

At that moment, Lionel looks up at the back of the boathouse and sees Natalie II coming out from behind a large boat. She is very pale. She obviously has not left the boathouse since the night before. She comes toward them, her eyes fixed on Patrice.

LIONEL: You were here? *(She does not answer him and goes up to Patrice.)* He's got a nasty wound. It was an accident . . . I'll explain it all to you.

NATALIE II *(looking at her brother):* I'm not asking anything of you, Lionel.

PATRICE *(moaning):* Natalie . . .

The brother and sister look at each other.

LIONEL: Please, go and help Anne. Hurry up. *(Natalie II leaves.)* Be patient, old man . . . Anne's on her way . . . She'll look after you . . . She'll make you better . . .

In front of the boathouse. Evening.

The wind has risen. The sea is very rough. Natalie II is sitting on a large stone, leaning against the boathouse, her hair blowing in the wind, staring straight ahead. She has an oilskin over her shoulders.

Anne comes out of the boathouse and goes up to her.

ANNE: I'm going back to the house. He still has a high fever. The blood is poisoned. It's a nasty wound, there's no use in lying to you . . . It got infected in the marsh. *(Natalie II puts her head in her hands.)* Ah! Don't cry!

She lifts up her head and looks at Anne without shedding a tear. She stands up.

NATALIE II: But I'm not crying!

The boathouse.

Lionel is leaning over Patrice, changing the compress on his forehead. Patrice is in a great sweat and talking feverishly.

PATRICE *(in a low voice):* Lionel . . .

LIONEL: You musn't talk.

PATRICE: Yes . . . yes . . . Lionel. Listen, come closer . . . I'm afraid of not being able to speak later. My head is swollen and throbbing . . . throbbing . . .

LIONEL: Well then, tell me.

PATRICE: Lionel, I know I'm very ill.

LIONEL: It won't last.

PATRICE: No, I'm very ill . . . listen . . . I must see Natalie again . . .
I must see her again.

LIONEL: Calm down now . . . calm down!

*They do not notice that Natalie II is listening through the wooden
boards of the boathouse.*

PATRICE: I must see her again . . . I won't calm down . . . I must . . .
I must . . .

LIONEL: Keep calm . . .

PATRICE: I shall keep calm when I've seen her again . . . You're my
brother, Lionel, you must fetch Natalie. You must tell her that
I'm very ill. You must go and fetch her. *(Patrice is becoming
more and more feverish.)* I don't want to die without seeing her
again . . .

LIONEL: Who's talking of dying?

PATRICE: I'm going to die, Lionel. And I want to see her again. You
must fetch her for me. If you refuse, I'll go!

LIONEL: You're mad!

PATRICE: Yes Lionel, I'm mad, I'm going mad. Listen to me, please
. . . please!

LIONEL: If you promise to be sensible I'll do anything you want.

PATRICE: Oh, thank you! Thank you, Lionel . . . *(He tries to sit up
and kiss his hand.)* You must leave at once . . . I don't want to
die without seeing her again . . . I don't want to, I can't . . . You
must tell my uncle, right away. He can't refuse, it's impossible
. . . She'd come to the ends of the earth . . . Lionel, when will
you leave?

LIONEL: Immediately.

PATRICE: Take the boat . . . I'll hear the engine . . . I'll recognize it . . . If you bring her back, take down the flag and put up one of her scarves, ask her for a white scarf . . . I'll see it from afar . . . Do you understand? Repeat it for me.

LIONEL: If I bring her back, I'll fly a white scarf from the mast.

Natalie II, who has heard all this, disappears.

In front of the boathouse.

Natalie II returns to where she was sitting earlier. She leans back against the wall and closes her eyes. Lionel comes out of the boathouse.

LIONEL: Watch over him, he's resting. I'm taking the boat. I have to inform his uncle.

NATALIE II: When will you be back?

LIONEL: Tonight or tomorrow morning . . . *(a little embarrassed)* I must hurry . . . You see, his uncle might hold it against me if I didn't let him know . . .

NATALIE II: Of course . . . go, then . . .

He kisses her and hurries off. Natalie II watches him leave and goes into the boathouse.

The boathouse.

Natalie II is leaning against the wall, far away from Patrice, who is talking deliriously. A lamp, swinging in the wind, lights up the scene. The shadows of the boats move on the walls. Patrice becomes agitated.

PATRICE: The sea! . . . It's on the sea . . . Don't you see anything on the sea?

NATALIE II: Keep calm, Patrice . . . keep calm. I'm here beside you.

PATRICE: Don't you see anything?

NATALIE II: It's night, Patrice, I can't see anything.

PATRICE *(propping himself up on his elbows):* Can't you hear anything? *(His head comes out of the shadows.)* Didn't you hear anything?

NATALIE II *(standing up and approaching him):* Hear what?

PATRICE: The sound of the engine . . . very far away. *(She puts a damp towel on his forehead. He listens carefully.)* Listen! . . .

NATALIE II: Don't get excited.

PATRICE: I can hear the engine.

She gently makes him lie down.

NATALIE II: Your ears are humming and you think you can hear it. *(She puts his arms under the blanket.)* If you really want to hear it, just lie down . . .

Patrice rests his head back.

Dawn.

Natalie II is still standing against the wall staring out at the sea.

PATRICE *(delirious):* Natalie! . . . are you there Natalie?

Natalie II does not move.

NATALIE II: Yes, Patrice, I'm here.

PATRICE: Can't you see anything on the sea? Can't you hear anything?

NATALIE II: No, Patrice, not yet . . .

Patrice tries to sit up, to look.

NATALIE II *(without leaving her post):* You'll exhaust yourself, Patrice . . . You're soaking wet.

PATRICE *(delirious):* The sea . . . the sea . . .

His hair is matted with perspiration. Natalie II suddenly hears the sound of a motorboat and looks out at the sea. Very far away, a boat is coming toward the island. Natalie II watches carefully . . . Patrice is fighting against death. The sweat is dripping from his forehead. Suddenly he hears the engine.

PATRICE: The boat . . . Natalie . . . the boat.

The boat is closer now. Natalie II sees a long white scarf flying from the mast.

PATRICE: Is it them? . . . Natalie? . . . the boat? . . .

NATALIE II: Yes . . . this time . . . it is.

PATRICE: Can you see it? . . . Answer me . . . Can you see it? Instead of the flag can you see a white scarf?

Natalie II, still staring at the sea, answers after a brief silence.

NATALIE II: No, I can see the red flag as usual. Why?

Patrice sits up, his face bathed in sweat, with a lost look in his eyes.

PATRICE: Look . . . again . . . *(entreating her)* Natalie . . . look . . . look . . .

NATALIE II *(turning around with cold anger):* It's the usual flag. The red one! *(Patrice falls back.)* Patrice!

NATALIE II *(running and throwing herself on him):* It's not true . . . Patrice! . . . It's not true . . . I lied . . . It's the white scarf!

She sobs. Patrice's eyes mist over. He tries to talk.

PATRICE *(murmuring):* I can't hold . . . on . . . any longer . . .

He dies. Natalie II moves back, with a shattered expression.

NATALIE II *(shouting):* Patrice!

Panic-stricken, she walks away from him, without taking her eyes off him. Then she runs to the door.

In front of the boathouse.

Natalie II comes running out. She suddenly stops. She has just seen Natalie coming up to the boathouse, helped by Marc, while Lionel ties up the boat. Natalie is walking with great difficulty.

MARC: You're exhausted . . .

NATALIE: Marc . . . let me go alone . . .

MARC: You'll never have enough strength.

NATALIE *(laughing nervously):* Me?

She stands up. Marc lets her go on alone. She goes to the boathouse as though she had wings. Her feet hardly touch the ground. Her cape billows out behind her. She passes Natalie II without even seeing her, without stopping. Natalie II watches her and throws herself into Lionel's arms.

NATALIE II: Lionel! It's terrible!

The boathouse.

Natalie stops in the doorway and sees Patrice's dead body stretched out in the middle of the boathouse. Moulouk is lying at his feet. She walks over to Patrice and looks at his face. She caresses him and puts her cheek against his.

NATALIE: Patrice . . . Patrice . . . I'm here!

She lies down next to him and puts her head next to his. Marc and Lionel come into the boathouse. Marc goes forward, Lionel joins him and wants to go on ahead, but Marc stops him.

MARC: No one can reach them now.

The two bodies are lying next to each other.

Death has sculpted them, enfolded them, lifted them onto a royal shield. They are alone, enveloped in glory . . .

AND SO BEGINS THEIR REAL LIFE.

The End

Orphée *(1950)*

Credits

Screenplay	Jean Cocteau
Director	Jean Cocteau
Producer	André Paulvé
Music	Georges Auric
Director of Photography	Nicolas Hayer
Sets	D'Eaubonne
Costumes	Escoffier
Production Director	Emile Darbon

Cast:	
Orpheus	Jean Marais
Heurtebise	François Peirer
The Princess	Maria Casarès
Eurydice	Marie Dea
Cegestius	Edouard Dermithe
	and
	Henri Crémieux
	Gréco
	Roger Blin
	Pierre Bertin
	Jacques Varennes

Small-town café. Seven o'clock in the evening.

A street-corner café, facing a small square. It is similar to the "Flore" in Paris. An awning with the words "Café des Poètes" covers the terrace. A guitarist strums. Inside, it is smoky. Casually dressed young couples sit with their arms around each other; others write and talk. The tables are very crowded. The customers drink little and have been there awhile.

Orpheus sits alone in the back of the room. He gets up, calls the waiter, and pays. As he leaves, he turns his head and looks with everyone else toward the terrace. Through the window they see a large, black Rolls Royce come to a halt. The chauffeur jumps out and opens the door. The Princess gets out.

PRINCESS *(to the chauffeur):* Heurtebise! Help Mr. Cegestius cross the square.

She helps a casually dressed young man get down from the car. He is obviously very drunk.

CEGESTIUS *(shouting):* I'm not drunk!

PRINCESS: Yes, you are. . .

The chauffeur props up the young man with his arm. The Princess goes ahead toward the café. They catch up with her as she greets the people on the terrace.

Inside the café, Orpheus walks to the door as the Princess enters. He stands back to let her pass, and looks at her. The young man, struggling to prove he can walk unaided, bumps into Orpheus, looks at him uncertainly, and mutters insults.

The terrace.

Orpheus walks along the terrace and leaves. He turns around and looks back with a surprised expression. In a corner of the terrace near the bushes is a disheveled middle-aged man sitting with three young men in sweaters, leather sandals, and untidy hair.

THE MAN *(waving and shouting):* Orpheus!

ONE OF THE YOUNG MEN: You're crazy. . . .

He stands up. The others follow suit. They pick up their glasses and leave. Orpheus comes up to the table.

THE MAN: Come and sit down for a moment.

ORPHEUS *(sitting down):* As soon as I arrive there's an empty space. . . .

THE MAN *(smiling):* You've come to put your head into the lion's mouth. . .

ORPHEUS: I wanted to see what it was like.

THE MAN *(drinking):* What would you like to drink?

ORPHEUS: Nothing, thank you. I've just had one. It was a bitter experience. It's very brave of you to speak to me.

THE MAN: Oh well . . . I'm no longer in the rat race. I stopped writing twenty years ago. I had nothing new to offer. People respect my silence.

ORPHEUS: They probably think I have nothing new to offer and that a poet shouldn't become too famous. . .

THE MAN: They don't like you very much. . . . .

ORPHEUS: What you mean is that they hate me.

The man looks around and watches the beautiful woman and the drunken young man as they leave the café and walk along the terrace. The guitar music has been replaced by jazz.

ORPHEUS *(turning back to the man):* Who is that young drunkard who was so pleasant to me and who does not seem to scorn luxury?

THE MAN: That's Jacques Cegestius. A poet. He's eighteen years old and everyone adores him. The Princess with him runs a magazine which has just published his first poems.

ORPHEUS: The Princess is most beautiful and most elegant. . .

THE MAN: She is a stranger. She can't seem to do without our social sphere. *(picks up a magazine)* Here's her magazine.

ORPHEUS *(opening it):* I see only blank pages.

THE MAN: It's called *Nudism.*

ORPHEUS: That's ridiculous.

THE MAN: It would be more ridiculous if those pages were covered with ridiculous texts. The excessive is never ridiculous. Orpheus . . . your most serious defect is knowing just how far one can go.

ORPHEUS: The public likes me.

THE MAN: Ah, but they're the only ones.

Another corner of the terrace. The Princess and Cegestius are standing next to the writers who have shunned Orpheus.

A WRITER: They're talking about us.

ANOTHER WRITER: Apparently things are changing and they're publishing texts now.

THE PRINCESS: I've got his here . . . keep them. In the state he's in, he leaves his poems lying around everywhere.

CEGESTIUS *(snatching the papers from the young writer):* Give me that! You bastard! I'm going to smash your face in — I'm going to smash your face in!

THE PRINCESS: Will you keep quiet! I can't bear a scandal!

CEGESTIUS: Of course!

The fighting spreads from table to table. The chauffeur enters the phone booth and dials a number.

HEURTEBISE: Police? Café des Poètes . .. there's a fight . . .

The terrace. Orpheus and the Man.

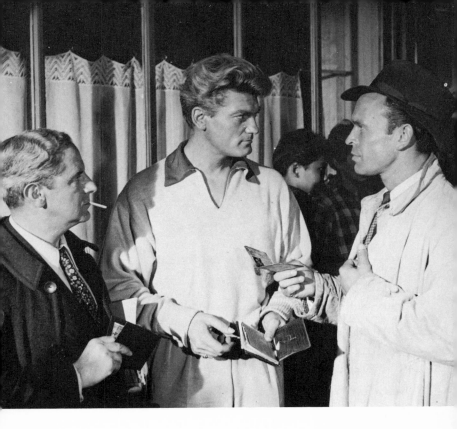

ORPHEUS *(bowing ironically):* Good-bye. Your café amuses me. You all think it's the center of the world.

THE MAN: It is. You know it's true and it upsets you.

ORPHEUS: Is my case hopeless, then?

THE MAN: No. If it were, you wouldn't arouse such hatred.

ORPHEUS: What should I do? Should I put up a fight?

THE MAN *(standing up):* Surprise us.

An expression of surprise suddenly appears on the man's face. Police cars arrive; gendarmes get out and enter the café amid the confusion of the fight.

POLICE: Your papers . . . papers . . .

Orpheus and the Man are still seated at the table.

FIRST POLICEMAN: Your papers. *(Orpheus takes his wallet from his pocket. The policeman looks at it and lifts his head.)* Excuse me, sir, I didn't recognize you, yet my wife has photos of you all over the place.

ORPHEUS: This gentleman is with me.

FIRST POLICEMAN: Please accept my apologies . . . *(saluting)* . . . Sir!

He moves away.

THE MAN: You get along too well with the police.

ORPHEUS: Me?

THE MAN: I'd advise you to get out of here as quickly as possible. They'll hold you responsible for this business.

ORPHEUS: Well!

The police are questioning the woman, the chauffeur, and several boys and girls. They are gesturing angrily.

CEGESTIUS: Leave me alone! Leave me alone!

PRINCESS: You have no right to touch that young man!

SECOND POLICEMAN: He doesn't have his papers. *(to Cegestius)* Follow us!

PRINCESS: I am responsible for him.

SECOND POLICEMAN: You can explain it all at the police station.

PRINCESS: This is inadmissible!

SECOND POLICEMAN: We are only carrying out our duty.

The young man struggles and shouts as they drag him away.

CEGESTIUS: Let me go, for Christ's sake, let me go!

They walk toward the square where the Rolls is parked.

CEGESTIUS *(shouting):* You rats! You swine! For Christ's sake, will you let me go! Let me go, will you!

They walk in confusion. Motorcycles can be heard in the distance.

A POLICEMAN: Oh, the pig! He bit me!

Cegestius escapes by ripping his sweater. Roar of the motorcycles. The policemen stop in their tracks, shouting.

POLICE: Watch out! Watch out!

Cegestius falls, flattened on the ground as though dropped from the sky. The two motorcycles roar away in a cloud of dust. The young man lies twisted in the dirt. The policemen look at the road and shout.

FIRST POLICEMAN: Did you get their numbers?

SECOND POLICEMAN: We couldn't see them.

FIRST POLICEMAN: Phone ahead along the road!

PRINCESS: Take him to my car, and see to all these wretched people. . . *(The young man is carried off.)* Heurtebise! Help them. . .

A group of people watch.

A YOUNG WRITER: To think that there's usually no one here!

Cegestius is hoisted into the car. The men and the chauffeur get out of the car.

PRINCESS *(turning):* Well, don't just stand there like a dummy!

Orpheus ventures forward with an inquiring expression, not certain if he is being addressed.

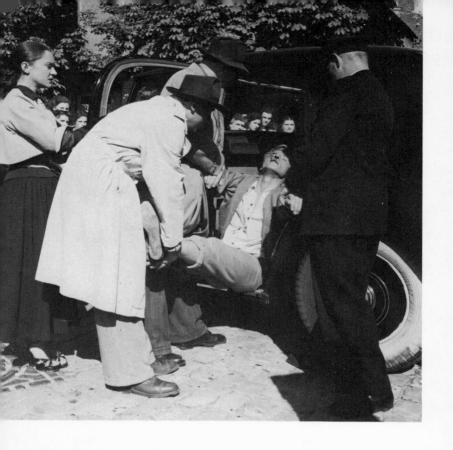

PRINCESS: Yes, you! You! Make yourself useful. *(turning toward Orpheus)* I need you as a witness. Get in! Quickly! *(getting into the car, shouting)* Come on! Come on! Hurry up!

Orpheus gets in after her. The door slams. The car moves off.

The car.

The people from the café stand outside the car. Inside is the body of the young man. There is blood at the corner of his mouth.

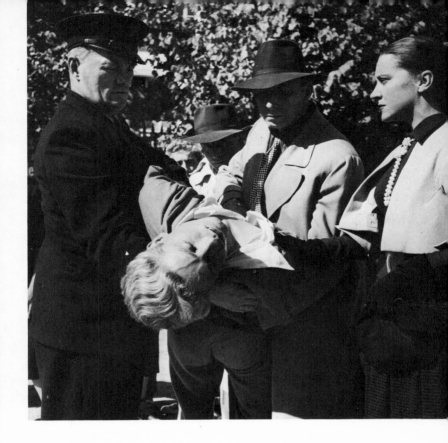

PRINCESS *(looking at Cegestius):* Give me your handkerchief.

Orpheus sits on the seat opposite her, looking at the evening landscape moving past the window. He hands her his handkerchief.

ORPHEUS: He looks badly wounded.

PRINCESS: Don't say such a pointless thing.

ORPHEUS: But we're going away from the hospital!

PRINCESS: You don't think I'm going to take this child to the hospital, do you. . .

The Princess wipes away the blood from Cegestius' face with the handkerchief. Orpheus lifts up Cegestius' eyelids.

PRINCESS' VOICE: Don't touch him!

ORPHEUS *(leaning back in amazement):* But . . . he's dead!

PRINCESS *(looking at Orpheus):* When will you learn to mind your own business? When will you learn not to meddle in other people's affairs?

She throws away her cigarette. The car brakes and stops at a level crossing.

ORPHEUS' VOICE: You asked me to get into your car . . .

PRINCESS' VOICE: Will you keep quiet . . .

Orpheus looks stunned. A train passes; the barrier is lifted. The car starts up again, accelerates, and crosses the tracks.

PRINCESS *(to the chauffeur):* Take the usual route. *(leaning toward the chauffeur)* The radio!

Heurtebise turns the radio knob. Sound of static, then a short-wave signal and Morse code.

THE RADIO: Silence moves faster when it's going backward. Three times. Silence moves faster when it's going backward. Three times. *(Morse code)*

The Princess listens carefully, leaning back against the cushions.

THE RADIO: Just one glass of water lights up the world . . . twice . . . Listen carefully. Just one glass of water lights up the world. Twice . . . Just one glass of water lights up the world. Twice . . . *(Morse code)*

ORPHEUS: Where are we going?

PRINCESS: Will you please keep quiet.

Roar of motorcycles. Their headlights approach the car, which has stopped. The Princess leans out a door.

PRINCESS *(shouting to passing motorcyclists):* Hello!

Orpheus watches the second motorcycle go by.

ORPHEUS: But they're the men who knocked the boy over.

PRINCESS: Don't be so stupid. And please don't ask me any more questions.

The car starts up again and drives away as the motorcycles cross in front of it on the road ahead.

The chalet. Night.

Two or three windows are lit up in the dark building. Sound of the motorcycles. The headlights of the car and the motorcycles move up the hill in a semicircle to the chalet. The motorcycles reach the chalet first. The riders get down and prop their machines against the wall. They go to the car. The chauffeur leaps out and opens the door. A train whistles.

PRINCESS *(to Orpheus):* Get down, and let my men see to him. *(She steps out between the motorcyclists.)* Take the body out of the car and carry him upstairs.

Orpheus gets out and looks behind him. The motorcyclists take the young man out, carrying him with his head hanging down.

Inside the chalet. Rubble.

PRINCESS *(going up the stairs):* Are you sleepwalking?

ORPHEUS: It feels like it.

The group comes up to a landing. They turn to their right, go down a few steps, and through an open door.

PRINCESS: You're all taking such a long time. I don't like that. *(to Orpheus)* Wait for me here.

Room with mirror.

The room is a shambles, as though just burglarized. There is straw on the floor. Furniture consists of an old table and some chairs. The wallpaper is torn. To the left of the door is a huge mirror. The windows and shutters are closed. The two motorcyclists enter carrying the body. The Princess follows them.

PRINCESS: Put him down on the floor.

She turns around and leaves. Orpheus waits on the landing, trying to see what is going on in the room. The Princess passes him.

PRINCESS: Follow me.

He follows her through a door on the right of the landing and up four steps to another door. The Princess opens it. Orpheus stops at the foot of the stairs. The Princess stands by the open door.

PRINCESS *(turning to Orpheus)*: You're really sleeping, aren't you. . .

ORPHEUS: Yes . . . yes . . . I'm sleeping . . . It's very strange.

Room with radio.

The room has a decadent elegance. It is furnished for a woman's comfort. Clothes and furs are hanging up or left lying around. Next to the shuttered window are a sofa, lamp, and radio. At the back of the room, left of the sofa, is a small door opening onto a brick corridor. In the opposite corner is a dressing table covered with bottles and brushes. Above the table is a three-sided mirror. The Princess switches on the lamp which throws a soft light into the room.

ORPHEUS: Please, Madam . . . will you explain . . .

PRINCESS: No, I won't. If you are sleeping and dreaming, accept your dreams. That's the role of the sleeper.

ORPHEUS: I have the right to ask for an explanation.

The Princess sits on the sofa and turns on the radio, which is playing a passage from Gluck's Orpheus (Eurydice's Complaint).

PRINCESS: You have every right, my dear Sir, and so do I. We are even.

She gets up and moves to her left.

ORPHEUS: Madam! Stop that music. In the room next door there is a dead man and the men that killed him. *(He turns the radio knob and stands up.)* Let me say again that I insist. . .

The Princess goes over to the dressing table and turns on the light over the mirror.

PRINCESS: And I insist that you leave that radio alone. Please sit down and keep quiet.

She sits down and arranges her hair. The mirror reflects the Princess and Orpheus standing by the radio.

THE RADIO *(emitting the same short-wave signal and voice heard in the car):* It would be better if mirrors reflected more. Once. I repeat. It would be better if mirrors reflected more. Once. It would be better if . . .

The mirror breaks, cracked along its entire length. The Princess leaps up while Orpheus stands next to the radio. Short-wave signal. The Princess walks abruptly to the radio and turns the knob. Music from Gluck's Orpheus.

PRINCESS: You are insufferable. *(She pushes Orpheus back onto the sofa.)* Wait for me here in my room. My servants *(Two Chinese servants in white jackets appear in the door of the brick corridor and bow.)* will bring you champagne and cigarettes. Make yourself at home. *(The servants bow and leave the room. The*

Princess walks quickly behind Orpheus toward the door. She stops.) You mustn't try too hard to understand what's happening, my dear Sir. It's a very serious mistake.

Orpheus sits next to the radio, which is still playing.

ORPHEUS: But Madam, I'm expected at home.

PRINCESS *(opening the door):* Let your wife wait for you. She'll be that much happier when she sees you.

She leaves the room and closes the door behind her. The servants bring in a champagne bucket and cigarettes on a cart. Orpheus stands up, then slowly sits down again, while one of the servants uncorks the bottle of champagne.

The room with the mirror.

The two motorcyclists are standing on either side of the mirror. The body of the young man is lying on the floor. The Princess quickly enters the room, walks over to the body and looks at it.

PRINCESS: Is everything ready?

ONE OF THE MOTORCYCLISTS: Yes, Madam.

(The action in the following scene is depicted through reversed film.)

Cegestius is standing in front of the Princess and lets himself fall back. Her hands reach out but do not touch him. He rises up slowly and stands in front of the Princess.

PRINCESS *(interrogating him):* Cegestius, stand up. *(Cegestius rises, his eyes wide open.)* Hello.

CEGESTIUS *(as though he were sleepwalking):* Hello.

PRINCESS: Do you know who I am?

CEGESTIUS: Yes, I do.

PRINCESS: Tell me.

CEGESTIUS: My death.

PRINCESS: Good. From now on you are at my service.

CEGESTIUS: I am at your service.

PRINCESS: You will carry out my orders.

CEGESTIUS: I will carry out your orders.

PRINCESS: Excellent. Well then, let's go. *(She turns toward the motorcyclists.)* Hold onto my dress. Don't be afraid. Don't let go of me.

She moves back with the young man just behind her. She goes quickly toward the mirror and passes through it with Cegestius. The mirror ripples like water. Orpheus stands, holding his glass of champagne, at the threshold of the door . . . The glass falls to the ground and breaks. The two motorcyclists follow the Princess and disappear into the rippling mirror, which turns back into an ordinary mirror again. Orpheus throws himself at it and hits it. His head sways, his hands slip, he collapses at the foot of the mirror.

Orpheus' head is reflected in the mirror. He appears to be at the foot of the mirror, but he is lying at the edge of a pool of water. White sand dunes meet the horizon. Orpheus moves as though he were waking up. He hoists himself onto his elbow and looks around in amazement. He climbs up onto a mound of sand.

ORPHEUS *(calling out):* Hey there! Hey!

He goes down one slope, up another, and walks to a path between the bushes. The Rolls is waiting at the edge of the road. Orpheus runs down toward the car. The chauffeur is asleep. Orpheus shakes him.

ORPHEUS *(shouting):* Where are we? *(The chauffeur wakes up, rolls off the seat, and opens the door.)* I want to know where we are!

HEURTEBISE: I don't know, Sir. I was told to wait for you and to drive you back.

ORPHEUS: Where's the Princess? Where's the chalet?

HEURTEBISE: Would you care to get into the car, Sir?

Orpheus climbs in, without taking his eyes off Heurtebise. The chauffeur shuts the door and gets in. The car moves off.

Orpheus' living room. Day.

A comfortably furnished room with a small kitchen adjoining it. There are many books. The dining table is covered with magazines. At the back, on the left, a small door opens onto the garden. A ladder leads up through a trap door into Eurydice's and Orpheus' bedroom. Next to it is a sofa. Eurydice is sitting by the window, which looks onto the garden and the road. Aglaonice and the Chief of Police are beside her.

AGLAONICE *(talking on telephone):* Yes, she does . . . this woman lives at the Hotel des Thermes. Let me speak to the Manager.

She hands over the telephone to the Chief of Police.

The porter's office at the Hotel des Thermes.

PORTER *(to the Manager):* You're wanted on the phone, Sir.

Orpheus' living room.

CHIEF OF POLICE: This is the Chief of Police, here. I'm sorry to trouble you again. Have you made your inquiries? Hello, hello, hello . . . don't hang up. . .

The Hotel des Thermes.

THE MANAGER: I'm afraid I can only repeat what I said earlier. We have no woman here who fits your description and I haven't seen any Rolls Royce.

Orpheus' living room.

CHIEF OF POLICE: I'll come around to see you at two o'clock. Goodbye.

He hangs up. Eurydice is sitting. Aglaonice is standing.

CHIEF OF POLICE *(walking up and down):* It's incredible. Neither at the Fabius Hotel, nor at the Two Worlds Hotel!

EURYDICE: He'll never come back.

Aglaonice puts her hand on Eurydice's shoulder and shakes her gently.

AGLAONICE: Come now, keep calm. Men always come back, they're so absurd.

EURYDICE: But where is he? Where can he be?

AGLAONICE: There's no point in lying to you. He's with that woman.

EURYDICE *(standing up):* Oh no! No! I can't believe it. You, you, Sir, tell her it's not true! You know Orpheus. . .

CHIEF OF POLICE: Madam . . . Madam!

EURYDICE: Tell her it's not true! Tell her. . .

CHIEF OF POLICE: What can I say. You always seemed to be such a perfect couple. But men sometimes lose their heads. . .

EURYDICE *(turning her head to the wall):* My God! Oh my God!

CHIEF OF POLICE *(going over to Aglaonice):* What an unpleasant business.

AGLAONICE *(in a low voice):* Won't there be a scandal in the press?

CHIEF OF POLICE *(in a low voice):* No, no . . . I gave the strictest orders. In any case the reporters aren't aware of what's going on.

The bell rings. The Chief of Police starts.

AGLAONICE *(looking out of the window):* It's a reporter, my dear Sir.

EURYDICE *(leaning against the wall, crying):* Who is it?

She rushes to the door.

The garden.

The reporter pushes open the gate and enters the garden. Eurydice is standing in the doorway. The reporter stops in front of her.

REPORTER: Good-day, Madam. I'm from *The Sun*. Is your husband
at home?

EURYDICE: My husband can't see anyone. He's asleep.

REPORTER *(insolently):* Asleep. . ?

The Chief of Police comes up behind Eurydice.

EURYDICE: He worked all through the night.

CHIEF OF POLICE: I came to see him, but I didn't want to wake him.

REPORTER: Fine. Well, I'll be off. Can I give you a lift, Sir?

CHIEF OF POLICE: No thanks, I have my car with me.

EURYDICE: What is it you want to know?

REPORTER: I want to interview him about the young man's accident.
As he's not in the hospital his friends are worried about him;
they want to know where he is.

CHIEF OF POLICE: Everything's all right. I'll go down to the news
office myself.

REPORTER: Good-bye, Madam.

*He nods and leaves. Aglaonice is standing near the door. Eurydice
and the Chief of Police go back into the room.*

AGLAONICE: Well done!

EURYDICE: It's so awful. . .

CHIEF OF POLICE: Don't worry. I'll notify the paper.

Eurydice bursts into tears.

AGLAONICE *(comforting her):* Now, now . . . you must be brave.

Outside the house.

The reporter is snooping around the garden. Sound of a car approaching. The reporter slips away.

The Rolls Royce drives up and stops in front of the other side of the house. Orpheus gets out and talks to the chauffeur.

ORPHEUS: Follow me. Be as quiet as possible. I'll open the garage door.

Orpheus disappears through a small door into a stable, which has been converted into a garage. He opens the door. The Rolls drives slowly into the garage and stops next to Orpheus' small car. Orpheus shuts the door.

ORPHEUS: It's agreed then. *(He opens the door that leads into the garden.)* . . . My wife wouldn't understand what happened. . .

Orpheus walks toward the house. The reporter comes around the corner and stops him.

REPORTER: I'm from *The Sun*. So, you were asleep, were you?

ORPHEUS: What?

REPORTER: I'll let you sleep, Orpheus, I'll let you sleep. Sweet dreams!

ORPHEUS: Get the hell out of here!

REPORTER: My paper will appreciate your friendly attitude.

ORPHEUS: Good-bye. And get out.

REPORTER: You'll regret your rudeness.

ORPHEUS: I couldn't care less about the press.

REPORTER: That's new.

ORPHEUS: Yes, it is, isn't it?

He pushes his way past the reporter. Aglaonice, Eurydice, and the Chief of Police are standing by the window. Orpheus walks across the garden.

Inside the house.

AGLAONICE *(shouting):* Eurydice! Eurydice! It's him!

Orpheus comes up the steps. Eurydice rushes to the door. They meet in the doorway. She clings to him, crying.

EURYDICE: Oh my darling . . . my darling . . . at last!

As Orpheus embraces her, he sees Aglaonice and the Chief of Police.

ORPHEUS: What are you doing here?

AGLAONICE: You're too kind! It's quite natural, Orpheus, when you abandon your wife for her to appeal for help to those who love her.

EURYDICE: I was sick with worry. I called Aglaonice.

ORPHEUS: And the Chief of Police?

CHIEF OF POLICE: I don't know if you realize just how serious the situation is.

ORPHEUS: I do know that I come home and find the police here with a woman whom I forbade to set foot in the house!

EURYDICE *(coming up behind Orpheus):* Orpheus!

Aglaonice starts to leave, followed by the Chief of Police.

AGLAONICE *(turning):* Your behavior is really the limit. You may regret it. *(She goes to the door and turns around again.)* Are you coming, Sir? I think your presence here is as undesirable as mine.

ORPHEUS: Go on, go on, don't let me keep you!

CHIEF OF POLICE *(taking his hat):* I shall ask you to come to my office tomorrow. Good-bye, Madam.

They leave.

EURYDICE: Orpheus! Aglaonice is dangerous! Her women's league is very powerful . . . you're mad!

Sound of a car driving off.

ORPHEUS: I may very well be going mad. . .

EURYDICE: Where have you been?

ORPHEUS *(exploding):* Oh no! No! *(He walks up and down the room shouting.)* No questions, please. No questions!

Eurydice is stunned. There are tears in her eyes.

EURYDICE: It's the first time you've ever stayed out all night, it's only natural that I should ask you. . .

ORPHEUS: Nothing! I want nothing asked of me!

He pours himself a drink and downs it. He pours another.

EURYDICE: Orpheus! Orpheus! You never drink. . .

ORPHEUS: Well I'm drinking now, do you mind?

EURYDICE: And I was waiting for you to come back, I was waiting so that I could tell you some really important news. . .

Eurydice takes the baby's bootee she is knitting and shows it to Orpheus . . . He rushes toward the ladder that leads to the bedroom. Eurydice drops her knitting. As Orpheus walks past the armchair, he steps on the bootee without even seeing it.

ORPHEUS: I don't want to hear any news! Least of all important news! The only news I ever hear is bad news!

Orpheus goes toward the ladder.

EURYDICE'S VOICE: Orpheus!

ORPHEUS: Enough! I want to sleep. Sleep, do you hear?

He goes through the trap door, which slams shut behind him.

Music. Outside the house.

Orpheus climbs out the bedroom attic window at the back of the house and goes down the ladder. Heurtebise watches him and walks around to the front of the house. Orpheus enters the garage. Heurtebise goes into the living room.

Inside the house. Music (Gluck's Orpheus*).*

EURYDICE: Who are you?

Heurtebise stops at some distance from Eurydice.

HEURTEBISE: I brought your husband home.

EURYDICE: Where was he?

HEURTEBISE: I'm the chauffeur of the lady who took him in her car
    yesterday.

EURYDICE: Did he spend the night with her?

HEURTEBISE: No, my employer was carrying a wounded man. Your
    husband was at the scene of the accident. He got into the car.
    But my employer doesn't like people meddling in her affairs.

EURYDICE: So?

HEURTEBISE: So she left us on the road. Her other car was waiting for her near the chalet where she lives. She drove off with the sick man.

EURYDICE: What about my husband?

HEURTEBISE: I couldn't get the engine started so I waited until daybreak. Your husband slept in the car. He was very worried about you. . .

EURYDICE *(from the kitchen):* I wish I could believe you.

HEURTEBISE: I might lie to you if I were a real chauffeur, but I'm not.

EURYDICE: What are you then?

HEURTEBISE: A poor student. I took the job as a chauffeur two weeks ago. My name is Heurtebise.

EURYDICE: You're making me feel a little better. My husband . . . do you know him?

HEURTEBISE: Who doesn't?

EURYDICE *(returning to the living room):* My husband adores me, but we've just had an argument. I hardly knew him . . . he was drinking. . .

HEURTEBISE: You've dropped your knitting.

He picks up the baby's bootee.

EURYDICE: Thank you. *(With one hand she takes the bootee; with the other she gently touches her stomach.)* I was about to give him the great news. He wasn't even listening to me. He didn't see or hear anything. He stepped on the bootee without even realizing it.

HEURTEBISE: He must be very tired. You don't sleep very well in a car.

EURYDICE: It could be that. He shouted that he wanted to sleep. *(She goes toward the kitchen.)* You must be exhausted. I'll make you some coffee. *(As she talks, she turns on the gas and pours some water into a saucepan.)* Where are you meeting your employer? . . . I mean, the lady . . . Do sit down.

HEURTEBISE *(sitting down at the table):* I have no orders. I'll wait for her in town.

EURYDICE *(in front of the stove):* You can wait here if you like. There's a small room above the garage. I must say it's not ideal, but you could put your car next to ours and wait. . .

HEURTEBISE: Admit it; you want me to stay here because I'm connected with what happened yesterday — which doesn't prevent you from being a very charming person.

EURYDICE *(walking around the table):* You're wrong. I'm a very simple woman. *(She takes a cup and the sugar out of the cupboard and puts them on the table.)* You must understand that women with a background like mine have a lot to fear from certain people.

HEURTEBISE: Your husband isn't the sort to lose his head.

EURYDICE: He's very handsome and very famous. It's a miracle that he's faithful to me. *(The water boils over and puts out the flame. Eurydice lets out a cry and runs to the kitchen.)* Oh, the water! *(She takes a rag, kneels down, and wipes the floor.)* I am stupid. Please forgive me.

HEURTEBISE *(close-up):* Hey! The gas!

EURYDICE: What?

HEURTEBISE: It's still on, be careful. *(Eurydice hears the hissing of the gas. She gets up, turns it off, strikes a match, and lights it again. There is a popping noise.)* I can't stand the smell and for a good reason too. . .

EURYDICE: What reason?

HEURTEBISE: I committed suicide by gas. The smell has been following me ever since I died.

EURYDICE: Since you died?

HEURTEBISE: Well . . . I mean since I almost committed suicide.

EURYDICE: Ah, I see. You don't look like a ghost.

HEURTEBISE: I was in love with an awful-looking girl. Pity she didn't look like you. Your name is Eurydice, isn't it?

EURYDICE: Indeed. I'm afraid I've forgotten yours.

HEURTEBISE: Heurtebise, at your service.

Music from Gluck's Orpheus *stops.*

The garage.

Orpheus is inside the Rolls Royce, listening to the radio and taking notes on a pad. The car door is open.

THE RADIO: The bird sings with its fingers. Twice. The bird sings with its fingers. Twice. I repeat. The bird sings with its fingers. . .

Orpheus' and Eurydice's bedroom. Night. Music.

Moonlight shines through the window. Twin beds are reflected in the three-sided mirror. Eurydice is sleeping in the bed on the right; Orpheus on the left. The light changes. The Princess comes through the mirror and walks over to the beds. She stands and looks at the dreaming Orpheus.

AUTHOR'S VOICE: That first night, the Death of Orpheus came to his room to watch him sleep. *(The light surrounding the Princess touches Eurydice's bed.)* The next day. . .

End of music.

The garage. Sunlight and shadows.

Orpheus is sitting in the front seat with his papers in his hand. Eurydice is sitting in the back. Heurtebise is leaning on the open door of the car.

EURYDICE: You don't have to sit in a car to listen to the radio.

ORPHEUS: I can't get this station anywhere else.

EURYDICE: Well, if I want the pleasure of your company, I see I shall have to live in a car.

ORPHEUS: No one's forcing you!

He turns the radio knob. Sound of music.

EURYDICE: Listen, darling. . .

ORPHEUS *(annoyed):* Ssh! *(Short-wave signal. Orpheus listens; Eurydice looks at Heurtebise in despair. Heurtebise signals Eurydice to keep quiet.)* I've heard nothing but meaningless sentences, except for one yesterday, which was marvelous.

HEURTEBISE: Why don't you rest for a moment. . .

ORPHEUS: Thanks! And the sentences will start up again as soon as I turn my back!

EURYDICE: Orpheus, you can't spend the rest of your life in a talking car. It's irresponsible of you.

ORPHEUS *(turning toward Eurydice):* Irresponsible? My life was beginning to fester, to stink of success and death. Can't you see that the most insignificant of these sentences is more amazing than all of my poems? I would give my whole life's work for one

of these sentences. I'm in pursuit of the unknown.

EURYDICE: Orpheus, we can't bring up our child on these little sentences.

ORPHEUS: Just like a woman, Heurtebise. You discover the world and they talk to you about taxes and baby clothes.

HEURTEBISE: I admire Orpheus. As for myself, I could hear these little sentences a thousand times without paying the slightest attention to them.

ORPHEUS: Where could they be coming from, Heurtebise? No other station broadcasts them. I feel certain that they are addressed to me personally.

EURYDICE: Orpheus! This car is the only thing that matters to you. I could die and you wouldn't even notice.

ORPHEUS: We were dead without even noticing it.

HEURTEBISE: Beware of sirens.

ORPHEUS: It is I that charms them.

HEURTEBISE: Your voice is the best one. Be happy with your voice.

ORPHEUS *(leaning closer to the radio):* Ssh!

THE RADIO: I repeat. 2294 twice. 7777 twice. 3398 three times. I repeat. 2294 twice. 7777 twice. 3398 three times.

Short-wave signal. Orpheus takes notes.

EURYDICE: Well, that's most poetic, I must say!

ORPHEUS: Who are we to say what is poetic and what isn't? *(He sits up.)* Anyway, if you're not happy you can go. I just want to be left in peace, that's all.

HEURTEBISE: Come on, Eurydice.

ORPHEUS: Take her away, she's driving me crazy!

EURYDICE *(getting out of the car):* It's this car that's driving you crazy!

ORPHEUS *(angrily):* Oh!

Heurtebise helps Eurydice out of the car and takes her to the house.

ORPHEUS *(shouting):* Take her away, Heurtebise, or I'll do something I'll regret.

Orpheus' bedroom.

Heurtebise and Eurydice come through the trap door.

EURYDICE: Orpheus is behaving atrociously.

HEURTEBISE: No . . . he's a genius and all geniuses have their whims.

EURYDICE: It's not the fact that he listens to the car that worries me . . . it's what he's really looking for. . .

HEURTEBISE: His attitude toward that woman won't change . . . he's interested only in the sentences.

EURYDICE: I know I'm being silly, but I'm very sensitive about these things. It's the first time that Orpheus has ever treated me like a dog.

HEURTEBISE: You mustn't exaggerate. It's just a little family row.

EURYDICE: It always starts with just a little family row.

HEURTEBISE: You must lie down and rest.

The phone rings.

EURYDICE: Would you answer it for me? *(She closes her eyes.)*

The living room.

Heurtebise answers the phone.

HEURTEBISE: Yes . . . this is Orpheus' home. No. It isn't Orpheus. Yes . . . yes . . . fine, Sir . . . I'll give him the message.

Heurtebise disappears. The receiver replaces itself on the telephone.

In front of the garage.

Heurtebise reappears. Orpheus comes out of the garage and approaches him.

HEURTEBISE: The Chief of Police phoned. He's waiting for you in his office. Your wife is resting; she doesn't feel well.

ORPHEUS: Well, that's normal in her condition.

HEURTEBISE: Go and see her . . .

ORPHEUS: All right. Would you get the car out? You can drive me to the police station.

HEURTEBISE: Mine?

ORPHEUS: No, mine. No one must suspect that the other one is here. The whole town would know.

Orpheus walks away. Heurtebise watches him and goes into the garage.

The garage.

The roar of motorcycles. Heurtebise rushes to the door and opens it. The motorcycles drive out at top speed.

The bedroom.

Eurydice is lying on her bed. Orpheus kisses her.

ORPHEUS: What's the matter? Don't you feel well?

EURYDICE: I feel fine.

ORPHEUS: Do you want me to get you a nurse?

EURYDICE: A nurse?

ORPHEUS: I can't leave you here alone.

EURYDICE *(smiling):* I won't be alone.

ORPHEUS: Don't be surprised at my bad mood. I've been resting on my laurels . . . it's essential that I wake up.

EURYDICE: Come back quickly.

ORPHEUS: Do you forgive me? My nerves are bad.

He goes down through the trap door.

In front of the garage.

Heurtebise drives out Orpheus' car and parks it at the side of the road. He gets out to close the garage door. Orpheus walks through the garden toward the car. Just as he turns around to look for Heurtebise, the garage door slams. Orpheus leaps back.

HEURTEBISE: What's the matter? Did I startle you?

ORPHEUS: My nerves are really on edge. I don't think I could drive myself.

HEURTEBISE: Aren't you afraid that they'll recognize me if I take you?

ORPHEUS *(getting into the car):* You can drop me there and wait some distance from the area so you won't be recognized.

The car drives off.

A road.

The car drives up and stops at the foot of some steps leading to a row of houses and a gas lamp.

ORPHEUS *(getting out of the car):* I'll go to the police station and come back right away.

HEURTEBISE *(laughing):* One can never be certain of coming right back from the police station.

ORPHEUS: You're very encouraging!

He starts up the steps.

At the top of the stairs. Music.

Orpheus walks up to the middle of Bolivar Square. A little girl is jumping rope. Orpheus stops and looks toward the road, past the fort-like buildings surrounding the square. The Princess is walking along the road. She vanishes through a doorway. Orpheus rushes along the road after her. He comes out among the arcades of the Place des Vosges. There is no one there. As he comes out from under one of the arches, he sees the Princess walking through another arch further on. She looks at her watch and continues walking through the arches. He runs after her, but all the archways are empty. When he reaches the end of the arcade he turns the corner and finds himself in the covered market at Boulogne. Some hikers stop a truck that almost runs over Orpheus.

ORPHEUS *(to the hikers):* You haven't seen a dark-haired young woman go by, have you?

One of the hikers answers in Swedish. The truck drives off. As Orpheus looks around, the Princess appears. She walks through the empty stalls. Orpheus rushes after her. He bumps into a cyclist who is pushing his bicycle and carrying a ladder on his back.

THE CYCLIST: Well, Mr. Orpheus, having some trouble, are you?

Orpheus shoves past him and runs down to the end of the row of

stalls. A couple is leaning against a fence kissing.

ORPHEUS: Excuse me...

They are too deeply engrossed in each other to take any notice of him. He crosses the market place. A fat woman is piling up some crates.

ORPHEUS: You didn't see a young woman go by, did you?

THE FAT WOMAN: Well now, Mr. Orpheus, chasing girls are you?

ORPHEUS: A very slim, elegant young woman who was walking very quickly.

THE FAT WOMAN: It was me.

She bursts out laughing. Orpheus continues on his way. He comes to the entrance gates of the market.

A YOUNG GIRL *(rushing up to him):* Mr. Orpheus, can I have your autograph please?

ORPHEUS: I have nothing to write with.

THE YOUNG GIRL: Monica! Give me your pen.

A crowd of young girls surrounds Orpheus and grabs at his clothes. He struggles. On the other side of the road the Princess gets into a car and starts the engine.

ORPHEUS: Let me go! Let me go!

THE GIRLS: Give us your autograph . . . Sign my exercise book . . . Sign my work card . . . Be a sport. . .

ORPHEUS *(shouting):* Let me go!

THE GIRLS: He's not so good-looking close-up . . . That's not him! . . . Yes it is, it is!. . . It's him!. . . It's him! . . . Sign! . . . Sign!. . .

The car drives off. Orpheus is struggling with the group of girls.

THE GIRLS: Sign! . . . Sign here! . . . Here!

Orpheus breaks away from the girls and rushes after the car.

ONE OF THE GIRLS *(shouting):* You fool!

ANOTHER YOUNG GIRL *(coming out of the café opposite waving a newspaper):* Here! Here . . . come quickly! He's in trouble! Read this.

The girls bury their heads in the paper.

In the police station.

The Chief of Police is holding a newspaper. He puts it down. Sitting in front of his desk are the middle-aged man from the Café des Poètes, the reporter, two writers, Aglaonice, and one of her young women.

CHIEF OF POLICE: A most unfortunate article . . . *(uproar)* You must all speak in turn, otherwise we'll never get anything settled. You were saying, my dear Sir, that this sentence is a poem. That's your affair. I am completely open-minded about it. You may speak.

THE MAN: Orpheus sent me these texts yesterday morning. I found them quite amazing. I showed them to some friends. . .

FIRST WRITER: And I noticed that one of the texts, which was rather astonishing I must admit, reminded me of something.

CHIEF OF POLICE *(looking at his papers):* It was, if I'm not mistaken, the text: "The bird sings with its fingers." I quote this without committing myself.

FIRST WRITER: The boy was a bit drunk the day of the accident.

CHIEF OF POLICE: You are referring to the victim, aren't you?

FIRST WRITER: Yes, Jacques Cegestius. He was supposed to give us a poem. I picked up the papers from the floor of the Café des Poètes the day of the fight. He wrote the sentence that you're looking at.

THE MAN: Orpheus didn't know Cegestius. He was sitting at my table. He saw him for the first time. The young man disappeared under tragic circumstances. And his sentence comes back to us through Orpheus, who was in the car and who maintains that he doesn't know what happened to Cegestius.

CHIEF OF POLICE *(to Aglaonice):* Madam, you run a woman's club, "The Bacchantes," don't you? I believe you can drink there till the early hours of the morning.

AGLAONICE: Yes, Sir, that's right, we serve champagne.

CHIEF OF POLICE: What do you have to say?

AGLAONICE: Orpheus married one of my waitresses. We were very fond of her. When she's upset she turns to us. She admitted that she was very unhappy.

CHIEF OF POLICE: Ladies and gentlemen, I don't for a moment doubt your good faith, nor your desire to come to the aid of justice. But there really isn't enough evidence to accuse one of our national heroes, Orpheus! Don't forget that at this moment the municipal brass band is named after him!

FIRST WRITER *(standing up):* We don't give a damn about national heroes, we will dispense our own justice.

He goes toward the door. The Chief of Police walks around the desk and follows him.

CHIEF OF POLICE: I've asked Orpheus to come and see me. He'll be here any minute now. I'm sure he'll have an explanation. . .

THE MAN: If the law refuses to intervene we will intervene ourselves. *(He nods his head.)* Sir!

He leaves, followed by the writers and Aglaonice.

CHIEF OF POLICE *(running after them):* Gentlemen! Gentlemen! Ladies!

The door slams shut.

The steps leading to Bolivar Square.

Orpheus goes to the car. Heurtebise is reading a newspaper. Orpheus gets into the car. Heurtebise gives him the paper.

HEURTEBISE: Have you read the article?

ORPHEUS: No, and I'm not going to.

He throws the newspaper away.

HEURTEBISE: You are quite right, it's disgraceful.

ORPHEUS *(while Heurtebise starts the engine):* Don't mention it to my wife, whatever you do.

HEURTEBISE: Did you meet a lot of people?

ORPHEUS: No, in fact the streets seemed to be particularly empty. I met some girls who wanted my autograph. And you?

HEURTEBISE: No one. Oh yes! My employer. She drove past in a little convertible. She slowed down, asked me if the Rolls was at your house, and told me to wait for her there.

ORPHEUS: You should have run after her and told her to stop!

HEURTEBISE: It is not the role of a chauffeur to give orders. Instead, the role of a chauffeur consists of accepting them.

ORPHEUS: Did she give you any?

HEURTEBISE: No, she told me to wait until I saw her at your house. What did the Chief of Police have to say to you?

ORPHEUS: I didn't go to the police station.

The car drives away.

Orpheus' bedroom. Night

The Death of Orpheus stands at the foot of the bed, with eyes painted on her eyelids.

THE AUTHOR'S VOICE: And every night, the Death of Orpheus returned to the room.

Orpheus' living room.

HEURTEBISE: No, Eurydice, no. . .

EURYDICE: I'm going, Heurtebise. I'm going to see Aglaonice. I must. She alone can advise me.

HEURTEBISE: Orpheus would hate you to do that.

EURYDICE: Orpheus couldn't care less about anything that isn't connected with that woman's car.

HEURTEBISE: And even if I agreed to drive you into town, Orpheus is in the garage; he'd see us leave.

EURYDICE: I'll go by bicycle. I'm used to it.

HEURTEBISE: That's ridiculous in your condition.

EURYDICE'S VOICE: I'm going!

HEURTEBISE: Eurydice! I know I have no right to forbid you . . . but if I implored you?

EURYDICE *(walking toward the door):* I'd go anyway. You won't stop me. It's driving me crazy.

She leaves.

HEURTEBISE *(in the doorway):* Aglaonice won't tell you anything, and you'll be exhausted. . .

He goes back inside. Motorcycles roar in the distance. Heurtebise goes to the window and looks outside with horror. The riderless motorcycles break to a halt with screeching tires in front of Orpheus' house. They disappear.

Garage.

Orpheus sits in the car, leaning close to the radio. Short-wave signal.

Orpheus' bedroom.

Heurtebise comes through the trap door carrying Eurydice's body and puts her down on the bed. The light changes. The Princess comes through the mirror, pushing the two sides like a door. The glow around her lights up the room.

PRINCESS: Come on, come on, Cegestius. You must get used to following me.

Cegestius comes through the mirror, holding a metal suitcase.

PRINCESS: Will you please close the doors.

CEGESTIUS: Which doors?

PRINCESS: The mirror. You never understand what you're told.

Cegestius closes the two sides of the mirror.

Cegestius and the Princess walk over to the bed where Heurtebise is standing guard.

PRINCESS: Hello!

HEURTEBISE: Hello.

PRINCESS: Is everything all right?

HEURTEBISE: Just about.

PRINCESS: What do you mean by that?

HEURTEBISE: Nothing, Madam.

PRINCESS: Good. I have a strong distaste for rebels.

HEURTEBISE: Yes, Madam.

PRINCESS: Well now, Cegestius. What are you making such a face for? Did you expect me to work with a shroud and scythe? My dear boy, if I appeared to the living as they imagine me to be, they would recognize me and it wouldn't make our task any easier. *(Cegestius walks over to the table.)* Heurtebise will help you. You'll never manage alone. I see I'll have to draw the curtains myself, since neither of you has thought of doing so.

(She closes the curtains.) Take everything off the table except the transmitter. *(darkness)* Cegestius, send out the messages. Come on, come on, get with it. You're obviously unaccustomed to not drinking. We've got no time to waste. *(The Princess projects light.)*

Cegestius stands in front of the table, turning the transmitter knobs. The Princess comes over.

CEGESTIUS *(Voice of the Radio):* The black crepe of little widows is a real sunshine meal. Twice. The black crepe of little widows is a real sunshine meal. Twice. I repeat. The black crepe of little widows. . .

PRINCESS *(ironically, walking toward Cegestius):* You really do find the most delightful sentences! Where are my gloves?

HEURTEBISE: They're not in the bag.

The sentences continue, followed by numbers: "5-5-7-2-3-7-3-5-5-7-12. I repeat . . ." etc., and the sound of Morse code.

PRINCESS *(to Cegestius):* Did you forget them? That would really be the limit!

CEGESTIUS: I'm sorry, Madam. I hope that you will forgive me.

PRINCESS: I knew it. Give me yours. *(Cegestius hands her his rubber gloves.)* Quick . . . quick . . . to your places. You know I insist on total discipline as though we were on board ship.

She walks around the bed as she puts on the gloves. Eurydice is lying there, motionless, lit up by the glow of the transmitter.

HEURTEBISE: What are your orders?

PRINCESS *(taking off her gloves):* I beg your pardon?

HEURTEBISE: I want to know if you have any orders.

PRINCESS: When I carry out orders I have been given I expect others to carry out mine.

HEURTEBISE: That's why I'm asking you if you were given any orders.

PRINCESS: How dare you!

HEURTEBISE: If you had specific orders your killers would have completed the job.

PRINCESS: Would you happen to be in love with that silly girl?

HEURTEBISE: And if I were?

PRINCESS: You are not free to love, neither in this world nor in the other.

HEURTEBISE: Nor are you.

PRINCESS *(coming up angrily to Heurtebise):* What?

HEURTEBISE: There can be no exception to the rules.

PRINCESS: I command you to be quiet!

HEURTEBISE: You're in love with Orpheus and you don't know what to do about it.

PRINCESS: Shut up!

Her dress turns white.

HEURTEBISE *(making an angry gesture):* I . . .

He disappears.

The Princess walks up to Cegestius, who is standing next to the table. Her dress turns black again.

PRINCESS: Send out the messages! Send out the messages! Just say anything.

CEGESTIUS *(turning round):* Madam . . . will I be able to disappear and reappear like Heurtebise?

PRINCESS: You are too clumsy! The messages!

CEGESTIUS *(Voice of the Radio):* Jupiter gives wisdom to those whom he wishes to lose. I repeat. Jupiter...

The garage.

Orpheus' face is near the radio; his hand on the knob.

THE RADIO: Jupiter gives wisdom to those whom he wishes to lose. Three times. Jupiter gives wisdom to those whom he wishes to lose. Listen carefully. *(Morse code. The sentences continue during the following conversation.)* The night sky is a hedgerow in May...

Heurtebise is standing by the door of the car.

HEURTEBISE: Orpheus! Orpheus!

ORPHEUS: Won't I ever be left in peace!

Orpheus turns toward Heurtebise, who is still standing by the car door.

HEURTEBISE: Your wife is in great danger. Follow me.

RADIO: The night sky is a hedgerow in May. I repeat. The night sky...

ORPHEUS *(grabbing his papers and taking notes):* Be quiet!

HEURTEBISE: I'm telling you that your wife is in great danger.

ORPHEUS: You're preventing me from listening...

HEURTEBISE: Do you hear me?

ORPHEUS: Wait till I've written this down.

He writes "hedgerow in May."

HEURTEBISE *(shouting):* Your wife is dying!

ORPHEUS: You just don't know her. She's play-acting to make me come home.

Heurtebise leaves.

Orpheus' bedroom.

The Princess is standing at the head of Eurydice's bed. She is removing a metal band from Eurydice's neck.

(The action in the following scene is depicted through reversed film.)

PRINCESS: Stand up.

Eurydice gets off the bed and stands in front of the Princess.

PRINCESS: You know who I am, don't you?

EURYDICE *(speaking in a strange, distant voice):* Yes.

PRINCESS: Tell me.

The trap door opens. Heurtebise pushes it back and stands on the steps of the ladder.

EURYDICE'S VOICE: My death.

PRINCESS' VOICE: From now on you belong to the other world.

EURYDICE: From now on I belong to the other world.

PRINCESS: You will obey my commands.

EURYDICE: I will obey.

PRINCESS: That's fine. *(to Heurtebise)* Ah, there you are! Orpheus must have refused to follow you.

HEURTEBISE: I'll talk about that . . . elsewhere.

PRINCESS: And I'll talk too. I have quite a lot to say.

She walks past the motionless Eurydice, toward Cegestius. She takes off her gloves and throws them on Orpheus' bed. She reaches

Cegestius as he fastens the suitcase.

PRINCESS: Don't forget my equipment, will you! *(Cegestius reopens the suitcase.)* Good. *(She turns toward Heurtebise.)* I suppose, Heurtebise, that you wish to remain on earth. You look just like a gravedigger standing in that trap door. You're quite ridiculous.

HEURTEBISE: I'm not the only one.

PRINCESS: I shan't forget your insults. Cegestius!

Cegestius walks around the bed and is astonished to see two Eurydices: one on the bed, one walking toward the Princess.

PRINCESS: Will you ever learn not to look back. Some people have been turned into pillars of salt playing that game.

She breaks the mirror with her fist. It shatters. Her dress turns white. The group goes through the broken mirror, which becomes solid again.

Heurtebise goes up to the mirror, which reflects his image. He turns around. The mirror shows him walking toward Eurydice, who is stretched out on the bed. He puts his hand on her forehead.

Orpheus comes out of the garage and closes the door behind him almost regretfully.

HEURTEBISE *(from the window)*: Orpheus! I warned you. You're too late . . .

ORPHEUS: Too late?

HEURTEBISE: Come up.

ORPHEUS: What are you doing in my room?

HEURTEBISE: Come in . . . through the window, which is so useful when you want to get out.

Orpheus climbs up the ladder. He goes into the room through the window and closes it behind him.

ORPHEUS: I asked you what you were doing in my room.

HEURTEBISE: Your wife . . .

ORPHEUS: What about my wife?

HEURTEBISE: Your wife is dead.

ORPHEUS: You're joking.

HEURTEBISE: It would be a very strange joke. You wouldn't listen to me.

ORPHEUS *(shouting):* Eurydice! Eurydice!

HEURTEBISE: Listen . . . listen to me, Orpheus.

Orpheus throws himself onto his knees in front of the bed.

ORPHEUS: Eurydice!

HEURTEBISE: It's too late to pity her.

ORPHEUS *(turning around toward Heurtebise with an anguished expression):* But how? How? Why?

HEURTEBISE: She fell down, but I think there's more to it than that . . .

ORPHEUS: What? What? *(He turns back to Eurydice.)* Eurydice! Eurydice! It's not possible! Look at me! Speak to me!

HEURTEBISE: There's still a way to redeem your folly.

ORPHEUS *(turning his head from side to side on the bed):* I'm still dreaming! It's the same nightmare! I know I'll wake up! Wake me up!

HEURTEBISE *(taking him by the shoulders):* Listen . . . listen to me . . . Will you listen to me? . . . Orpheus!

ORPHEUS *(raising his head):* It's hopeless.

HEURTEBISE: You've got one chance.

ORPHEUS *(bitterly):* What's that?

HEURTEBISE *(pulling him up onto his feet):* Orpheus! *(shaking him)* Orpheus! You have met Death.

ORPHEUS: I talked about it. I dreamed about it. I sang about it. I thought I knew it, but I didn't.

HEURTEBISE: You do . . . you know it personally.

ORPHEUS: Personally?

HEURTEBISE: You've been to her home.

ORPHEUS: To her home?

HEURTEBISE: In her very room . . .

ORPHEUS *(shouting):* The Princess! *(Heurtebise nods.)* My God! *(He tears himself away from Heurtebise and rushes over to the mirror.)* The mirror . . .

HEURTEBISE *(coming up to Orpheus):* I will tell you the greatest secret . . . Mirrors are the doors through which Death comes and goes. Besides, look at yourself in the mirror throughout your life and you will see Death at work like bees in a glass hive.

Orpheus touches the mirror and turns toward Heurtebise.

ORPHEUS: How do you know all these amazing things?

HEURTEBISE: Don't be naive. One doesn't work for my employer without finding out certain . . . amazing things.

ORPHEUS: Heurtebise! There's nothing we can do!

HEURTEBISE: We can join her.

ORPHEUS: But no man can . . . unless he kills himself.

HEURTEBISE: A poet is more than a man.

ORPHEUS: But my wife is there . . . dead . . . on her deathbed!

Orpheus turns around and runs to the head of the bed.

HEURTEBISE: That's only one of her forms, just as the Princess is a form of death. All that is false. Your wife is living in another world and I'm inviting you to follow me there.

ORPHEUS: I'll follow her all the way to Hades.

HEURTEBISE: We're not asking that much of you.

ORPHEUS: Heurtebise, I want to join Eurydice.

HEURTEBISE: You don't have to beg me. I'm offering it to you. *(putting his hands on Orpheus' shoulders)* Orpheus, look me in the eyes. Is it Eurydice you want to join, or Death?

ORPHEUS: But . . .

HEURTEBISE: I am asking you a very precise question; is it Eurydice you want to see, or Death?

ORPHEUS *(looking away):* Both of them . . .

HEURTEBISE: . . . and if you could, you'd cheat on one with the other . . .

ORPHEUS *(rushing toward the mirror):* Let's hurry.

HEURTEBISE: I congratulate myself on no longer being alive.

The Princess' gloves are on Orpheus' bed.

HEURTEBISE *(removing the gloves):* Someone left their gloves behind.

ORPHEUS: Gloves?

HEURTEBISE: Put them on . . . come on, come on . . . Put them on.

He throws the gloves at Orpheus. Orpheus catches them, hesitates

for a moment, and puts them on.

(The action in the following scene is shown through reversed film.)

HEURTEBISE *(standing by the mirror):* With those gloves you'll go
through the mirror as though it were water!

ORPHEUS: Prove it to me.

HEURTEBISE: Try it. I'll come with you. Look at the time.

*The clock shows just a second before six o'clock. Orpheus prepares
to go through the mirror. His hands are at his side.*

HEURTEBISE: Your hands first! *(Orpheus walks forward, his gloved
hands extended toward the mirror. His hands touch the*

reflected hands in the mirror.) Are you afraid?

ORPHEUS: No, but this mirror is just a mirror, and I see an unhappy man in it.

HEURTEBISE: It's not a question of understanding; it's a question of believing.

Orpheus walks through the mirror with his hands in front of him. The mirror shows the beginning of the Zone. Then the mirror reflects the room once more.

The garden gate.

The postman rings the bell at the garden gate. He rings again, looks around, and slips a letter through the slit in the mailbox. The letter slides through.

The Zone. Music.

A road surrounded by demolished buildings. Heurtebise is engulfed by a strong, silent wind.

ORPHEUS *(following Heurtebise):* Where are we?

HEURTEBISE *(walking stiffly):* Life takes a long time to die. This is the Zone. It consists of the memories of men and the ruins of their habits.

ORPHEUS: And do all the mirrors in the world lead to the Zone?

HEURTEBISE: I suppose so, but I don't want to put on airs. I really don't know much more than you.

Orpheus stops and looks around. Heurtebise walks on. However, it appears that the Zone is moving rather than Heurtebise.

HEURTEBISE *(turning around toward Orpheus without stopping):* Come on . . . come on.

ORPHEUS *(catching up with him):* I can hardly keep up with you. You look as though you're not moving.

HEURTEBISE: That's another story.

A glassmaker crosses the road behind Orpheus.

THE GLASSMAKER: Glass! New glass!

ORPHEUS: Who are all these people wandering around? Are they alive?

HEURTEBISE: They think they are. There is nothing as stubborn as professional enthusiasm.

ORPHEUS: Are we going far?

HEURTEBISE: Those words don't mean anything here.

ORPHEUS: There's no wind. Why do you look as though you're walking against the wind?

HEURTEBISE: Why? . . . always why! Don't ask me any more questions, just walk! Do I have to take you by the hand?

Heurtebise takes Orpheus by the hand and drags him along. They cross a large open space and go down some steps.

The chalet.

Room with the mirror. Night.

Three judges sit at the table. The Court Clerk is at the end of the table. Cegestius stands in front of the table, dressed as he was in the Café des Poètes. One of the motorcyclists guards the door leading into the corridor. The shutters are closed. The room is harshly lit. There are several documents on the table.

FIRST JUDGE: Were you ordered to send out messages?

CEGESTIUS: Yes.

FIRST JUDGE: Were you ordered to send out specific messages? Did you submit the texts beforehand? Answer carefully.

CEGESTIUS: No, I invented the sentences and numbers. I even transmitted sentences that I had written previously.

SECOND JUDGE: Did you notice anything particular about Heurtebise's attitude?

CEGESTIUS: No. I admired him for being able to disappear and reappear at will. I wanted to do that, but the Princess said I'd never be able to; I was too clumsy.

FIRST JUDGE: All right . . . all right.

He whispers something to the second judge.

SECOND JUDGE: Take this young man away and bring in the next person.

The first motorcyclist comes up to Cegestius, puts his hand on his shoulder, and leads him away. They go off toward the stairs. The Princess appears in the door opposite, followed by the second motorcyclist. She walks toward the table. The motorcyclist closes the door and takes his companion's place. The Princess stops in front of the table.

PRINCESS: May I sit down?

FIRST JUDGE: You may.

PRINCESS *(sitting down):* May I smoke?

FIRST JUDGE: If you wish.

The Princess takes out a cigarette and lights it. She puts her cigarette case and lighter down on the table.

FIRST JUDGE'S VOICE: You are accused of having taken away a woman without authority, of having devoted yourself to certain activities, of having shown initiative when you had only received orders . . .

SECOND JUDGE: Or at least permission . . . .

FIRST JUDGE: . . . to take a young man into your service. What do you have to say?

PRINCESS: Nothing. It was the result of a chain of circumstances.

SECOND JUDGE: It is not a matter of circumstances, it is a matter of orders. Did you receive orders?

PRINCESS: The other world is ruled by laws that are different from ours. I may have gone beyond the limits of my work without realizing it.

The judges confer in whispers.

FIRST JUDGE: Before continuing our inquiries, we shall await the appearance of another defendant and a witness.

SECOND MOTORCYCLIST: They're coming.

He touches the mirror. Orpheus jumps through it into the room, followed by Heurtebise. Orpheus starts back.

HEURTEBISE: We are just like rats . . .

PRINCESS: Hello! Do not be mistaken, my dear Sir, these are my judges. Just keep calm.

Orpheus looks at the Princess and goes up to the table. Heurtebise stands at his side.

FIRST JUDGE: Come closer.

Heurtebise moves closer.

PRINCESS: Well, Heurtebise! *(She puffs her cigarette and exhales.)* Now's the time to say what you have to.

HEURTEBISE: I have nothing to say.

SECOND JUDGE *(looking at his papers):* You are accused of having taken part in an intrigue in which this woman, without any superior order whatsoever, involved herself. Do you have a valid excuse?

HEURTEBISE: I was her assistant. I followed her.

FIRST JUDGE: You did, however, stay behind in the other world and were involved in human affairs, which you have no right to do.

The Princess stares at Heurtebise.

HEURTEBISE: Perhaps . . .

FIRST JUDGE: There is no "perhaps" here.

SECOND JUDGE: Please answer.

Orpheus moves back, and looks at the Princess.

HEURTEBISE: I didn't think I was disobeying . . .

FIRST JUDGE: Come closer.

Orpheus continues to look at the Princess.

FIRST JUDGE: You . . . you! . . .

ORPHEUS: Me?

FIRST JUDGE: Yes, you. Your name?

ORPHEUS: Orpheus.

FIRST JUDGE: Profession?

ORPHEUS: Poet.

The Court Clerk stops writing and looks up.

CLERK: His file says "writer."

ORPHEUS: It's almost the same thing.

SECOND JUDGE: There is no "almost" here. What do you mean by "poet"?

ORPHEUS: One who writes without being a writer.

The judges confer in low voices.

FIRST JUDGE *(facing the Princess):* Do you recognize this man?

PRINCESS: Yes.

FIRST JUDGE: Do you admit to having taken away his wife?

PRINCESS: Yes.

FIRST JUDGE: . . . So that you could get rid of her and try to have this man all to yourself?

ORPHEUS: Gentlemen!

CLERK: Silence!

PRINCESS *(to Orpheus):* Please be quiet, Sir. Just keep calm.

FIRST JUDGE: Do you love this man?

The Princess doesn't answer. She exhales. Orpheus starts.

FIRST JUDGE: Do you love this man?

PRINCESS: Yes.

FIRST JUDGE: Is it true that you went to his room and watched him sleep?

Silence.

PRINCESS: . . . Yes.

Orpheus is stunned.

SECOND JUDGE: Sign this please.

He leans over toward the Court Clerk, who hands him a document. The judge puts it on the table in front of the Princess. She stands up and walks over to Orpheus.

PRINCESS *(to Orpheus):* Do you have a pen? *(Silence. She laughs.)* I forgot that you weren't a writer.

She is given a pen. She signs the paper.

FIRST JUDGE *(rising):* Take these two people to the other room.

The motorcyclist leads the Princess away. Orpheus remains stunned.

The motorcyclist pushes him along. Heurtebise follows them. The first judge stops him.

FIRST JUDGE: Not you. You must stay.

The Princess, Orpheus, and the second motorcyclist go through the door. The first motorcyclist comes in and guards the door. Eurydice enters, as though sleepwalking. She stops in the doorway.

FIRST JUDGE: Come . . . come closer.

Eurydice approaches him and stops where the Princess had been standing.

FIRST JUDGE: Do you recognize this man?

EURYDICE *(turning her head toward Heurtebise):* Yes . . . that's Heurtebise.

FIRST JUDGE: Did he try to talk to you during your husband's absence? Did he say anything dubious?

EURYDICE *(opening her eyes wide):* Dubious? . . . Of course not . . . that's Heurtebise.

The judges confer.

FIRST JUDGE: Heurtebise, do you love this woman?

Silence. Eurydice stares at Heurtebise.

FIRST JUDGE: I repeat, Heurtebise, do you love this woman?

HEURTEBISE: Yes.

FIRST JUDGE: That is all we wish to know. Sign.

He gives Heurtebise a paper. Heurtebise signs.

The chalet. The room with the radio.

Orpheus and the Princess are in each other's arms in front of the sofa near the radio. They separate. They look into each other's eyes and talk in a low voice. Music.

ORPHEUS *(thrilled):* And you said yes . . .

PRINCESS: One can't lie here.

ORPHEUS: My darling . . .

PRINCESS: I loved you long before we first met.

ORPHEUS: I must have seemed so stupid . . .

PRINCESS: What is there to say? I have no right to be in love . . . yet I'm in love.

She kisses him. They separate. The Princess falls back onto the sofa. Orpheus gets down on his knees.

ORPHEUS: But you are all-powerful.

PRINCESS: You may think so. But here, there are countless faces of death, both young people and old, who receive orders . . .

ORPHEUS: And if you were to disobey? They can't kill you . . . It is you who kills . . .

PRINCESS: What they can do is far worse.

ORPHEUS: Where do these orders come from?

PRINCESS: They are transmitted by so many messengers that it's like the tom-tom of your African tribes, the echo of your mountains, the wind in the leaves of your forests.

ORPHEUS: I will find the one that gives these orders.

PRINCESS: My poor darling . . . he is nowhere. Some believe that his thoughts are with us, some that we are his thoughts. Others believe that he sleeps and that we are a dream, a bad dream.

ORPHEUS: I'll take you away from here. We are free.

PRINCESS: Free?

She laughs strangely and leans back against the cushions.

ORPHEUS *(moving down next to her):* I don't want to leave you.

PRINCESS: I must leave you, but I swear I'll find a way for us to be reunited.

ORPHEUS: Say "forever."

PRINCESS: Forever.

ORPHEUS: Swear to it.

PRINCESS: I swear.

ORPHEUS: But now . . . now?

PRINCESS *(sitting up):* Now? Their police are here.

ORPHEUS: If by some miracle . . .

PRINCESS: Miracles only happen in your world . . .

ORPHEUS: All worlds are moved by love.

PRINCESS: No one is moved in our world. Things proceed from tribunal to tribunal.

The music stops. Sound of the door opening. They separate and look around. One of the motorcyclists is standing in the doorway.

SECOND MOTORCYCLIST: Come with me.

The Princess and Orpheus stand up.

PRINCESS: Go . . . I love you; don't be afraid.

ORPHEUS: I don't want to lose you.

PRINCESS: If you resist, you'll lose us both.

SECOND MOTORCYCLIST: Follow me.

They walk toward the door and leave the room. The motorcyclist follows.

The Tribunal.

Heurtebise and Cegestius are sitting next to each other against the wall, facing the door. They stand up.

FIRST JUDGE *(rising):* After due consideration, we have reached the following verdict: The court of inquiry has decided to grant provisional freedom to the Death of Orpheus and her assistants. *(Cegestius, Heurtebise, the Princess, and Orpheus stand silently.)* Orpheus is free, on condition that he never reveals what he has seen. Eurydice is free to live in the other world, on condition that Orpheus never looks at her again. Just one look at her and he will lose her forever.

ORPHEUS: But . . .

COURT CLERK: Silence!

Eurydice is brought in by the first motorcyclist.

FIRST JUDGE: Here is your wife.

Orpheus turns his head but is stopped by a shout from Heurtebise.

HEURTEBISE: Be careful! *(Orpheus hides his face with his hand.)* Don't look at her . . .

The judge gathers up his papers. He leans toward Orpheus.

FIRST JUDGE: Not a very good beginning!

HEURTEBISE *(leaning forward on the table toward the Judge):* May I be allowed to accompany Orpheus to his home? I'm afraid that the condition you have imposed will be difficult for him to observe without assistance from one of us.

The judges stand up.

FIRST JUDGE: You may accompany the husband ... and wife. *(Bowing ironically to Heurtebise.)* With our kind permission, of course.

HEURTEBISE *(walking up to Orpheus):* Do you have the gloves?

ORPHEUS: No. Ah, yes! In my pocket.

HEURTEBISE: Put them on. Close your eyes. I'll guide you. It will be easier this way at first.

ORPHEUS: But her ... May I look at her?

HEURTEBISE *(in a low voice):* On no account whatsoever. Don't turn around. Don't open your eyes on any account. Come.

He takes Orpheus' hand and leads him away.

HEURTEBISE *(to Eurydice):* Hold him by the shoulders, it's safer. Come.

Eurydice, moving like a sleepwalker, comes up behind Orpheus and puts her hands on his shoulders. Orpheus does not move. Heurtebise walks around in front of him. He takes hold of Orpheus' and pulls him along. Eurydice follows. The Princess stands to the right of the empty table where the judges were sitting, with her hand on Cegestius' shoulder. Cegestius looks at her and then stares at the mirror.

CEGESTIUS: Where are the judges? *(vague gesture from the Princess)* The bastards!

PRINCESS: Cegestius ... if we were in our old world, I'd say to you "let's have a drink."

Orpheus' garden. The mailbox.

The letter slides through the slit and falls into the box behind the glass pane. The postman rings the bell, looks toward the house, and leaves.

The living room.

The clock chimes six o'clock. Orpheus comes down the ladder from the bedroom followed by Eurydice and Heurtebise.

ORPHEUS: What! Six o'clock? We went through the mirror at six o'clock.

HEURTEBISE: You promised you wouldn't talk about such matters.

EURYDICE *(herself again; looking toward the window):* There's a letter.

ORPHEUS: I'll go.

HEURTEBISE: Shout from the garden "I'm ready to come in" and Eurydice will hide.

ORPHEUS *(tightlipped):* How convenient!

EURYDICE: What a nightmare!

The garden. The door and the mailbox.

Orpheus takes the envelope from the box, opens it, and reads the letter.

The living room.

Eurydice walks over to the mirror on the wall above the sofa and looks at herself. Heurtebise is behind her.

HEURTEBISE: Watch out!

EURYDICE: Why shouldn't I look at myself?

HEURTEBISE: If Orpheus comes in, he might see you in the mirror.

EURYDICE: Thank goodness you came with us!

She moves away from the mirror.

HEURTEBISE: Eurydice, do you forgive me for what I said at the Tribunal?

EURYDICE: What was it you said?

ORPHEUS' VOICE *(from the garden):* Heurtebise!

Silence.

HEURTEBISE: Nothing, I'm sorry. *(He walks over to the door.)* When Orpheus comes in, hide behind the table.

The garden door.

Heurtebise goes down the steps. Orpheus is standing below.

ORPHEUS *(showing him the letter):* An anonymous letter! Written backward.

Orpheus comes up the steps.

HEURTEBISE *(turning and shouting):* Watch out Eurydice, watch out! He's coming in!

The living room.

Orpheus quickly enters with the letter in his hand. He walks over to the table and then toward the mirror.

HEURTEBISE *(rushing forward):* Be careful Orpheus! Eurydice, are you under the table?

EURYDICE'S VOICE: Yes.

Heurtebise goes to the table. Orpheus passes behind it and stands in front of the mirror. Eurydice lifts up the carpet in front of her and raises her head.

EURYDICE: Where is he?

ORPHEUS: Where are you?

HEURTEBISE: She's there . . . there, behind the table.

ORPHEUS: Ah! Everything's all right then.

He holds the letter up to the mirror. The reflection shows: "You are a thief and a murderer. Be prepared to meet your death."

HEURTEBISE: Beware of mirrors.

Both Orpheus and Heurtebise are reflected in the mirror.

ORPHEUS: You don't have to remind me.

HEURTEBISE: I was talking of your wife's reflection.

EURYDICE'S VOICE: Heurtebise has forbidden me to look at myself in the mirror.

As she speaks, Orpheus puts his finger to his lips and shows Heurtebise the letter. Heurtebise takes the letter, crumples it, and puts it in his pocket.

HEURTEBISE *(speaking in a low voice):* You must get rid of this letter, you fool.

Eurydice is crouching under the table, half hidden by the carpet. Orpheus and Heurtebise are standing behind the table.

EURYDICE: May I come out?

ORPHEUS *and* HEURTEBISE: No!

HEURTEBISE: Just a minute . . . *(to Orpheus)* Turn around . . . *(to Eurydice)* You may come out now.

Eurydice stands up.

ORPHEUS *(with his back turned to her):* This ridiculous situation demands the utmost care and attention. It will cause us a great deal of strain.

EURYDICE: It'll become a habit . . .

ORPHEUS: A strange habit, I must say!

EURYDICE: It's better than being blind or crippled . . .

ORPHEUS: In any case . . . we have no choice.

EURYDICE *(to Heurtebise):* It even has its advantages. Orpheus won't see me growing old and wrinkled.

ORPHEUS: Marvelous! You're really looking on the bright side of things.

HEURTEBISE: I don't see what else your wife could do.

ORPHEUS *(starting to turn around):* What else!

HEURTEBISE *(shouting):* Watch out!

Eurydice dives to the floor. Orpheus turns away with an obstinate and angry expression.

HEURTEBISE: You're living dangerously, my dear man.

ORPHEUS: I don't intend to go on living with my face glued to the wall, let me tell you.

EURYDICE: I'll get you a drink. Close your eyes. Heurtebise will help you sit down while I open the refrigerator.

She goes toward the kitchen. Heurtebise walks around the table and takes Orpheus by the hand. He sits him down, with his back to Eurydice.

ORPHEUS: I'll tell you what else my wife could do! She could try to understand exactly how difficult this is for me.

HEURTEBISE: Orpheus! And what about her? Don't you think she's suffering too?

ORPHEUS: You are quite wrong, my dear man. Women adore complications.

Orpheus is seated; Heurtebise stands by his side. Eurydice emerges from the kitchen, carrying a tray loaded with glasses, a bottle and ice.

EURYDICE *(as she walks):* Close your eyes.

ORPHEUS: Shall I tie a handkerchief around my head?

EURYDICE *(behind him):* No Orpheus, you'd only cheat. It's better to get into the habit from the beginning.

Orpheus closes his eyes and taps his fingers lightly on Heurtebise's arm as though to say "incredible!" Eurydice walks by him and puts down the tray.

EURYDICE: It's not easy, I must admit, but I'm sure we'll manage.

ORPHEUS: Bring up a chair and come and sit down. I'll turn my back.

He turns around and picks up a magazine from the table, opening it to an article entitled "The House of the Poet." It features two large photographs of Orpheus and Eurydice. Orpheus quickly closes the magazine, lifts his head and cries out.

ORPHEUS: Oh!

HEURTEBISE: Your wife's photo isn't your wife.

Orpheus puts his head in his hands. Eurydice sits down behind him.

EURYDICE: I'm exhausted . . .

ORPHEUS: We must make certain decisions right now, and it's up to me to make them. We can't spend the rest of our lives playing hide and seek.

EURYDICE: Do you want me to go and live somewhere else?

ORPHEUS: Why must you always exaggerate?

HEURTEBISE: Come now, Orpheus.

ORPHEUS: Well we can't possibly sleep in the same room. I shall sleep here, on the sofa.

EURYDICE: Now you're the one who's seeing the worst side of things.

ORPHEUS *(moving toward her):* Will you let me speak!

HEURTEBISE: Be careful!

He takes hold of Orpheus' head and turns him around.

ORPHEUS: It's her fault. She'd make a dead man turn around.

EURYDICE: I should have remained dead.

ORPHEUS: Be quiet! My nerves are in a dreadful state. I'm capable of doing just about anything!

HEURTEBISE: Orpheus, you've made your wife cry!

ORPHEUS: Since my presence is so disturbing, I'll leave!

He gets up and walks toward the ladder.

HEURTEBISE: Orpheus! Orpheus! Where are you going?

Orpheus climbs up the ladder and opens the trap door.

ORPHEUS: To my room.

He disappears. The trap door closes behind him. Eurydice collapses onto the table, burying her head in her arms.

HEURTEBISE: Relax . . .

He puts his hand on her arm.

Music. Gluck.

EURYDICE *(raising her head):* He hates me.

HEURTEBISE: If he hated you, he wouldn't have brought you back from death. He'll be held up as a wonderful example . . .

EURYDICE: He didn't do it for me . . .

HEURTEBISE: Eurydice!

EURYDICE: You know it, Heurtebise. You know where he's gone. To *her* car.

Night. The bedroom.

Eurydice, wearing a nightdress, opens the trap door and goes down the ladder. Orpheus is in a deep sleep on the sofa. Next to him, the lamp is still switched on.

Music.

THE AUTHOR'S VOICE: Eurydice felt she had lost Orpheus. She could not bear this situation. She wanted to free him, and there was only one way.

Eurydice goes up to the sofa. She leans over Orpheus. She puts out her hand, but does not dare touch him. Finally she shakes him gently.

EURYDICE *(in a low voice):* Orpheus! Orpheus!

Orpheus turns over toward the wall. Eurydice shakes him a little harder.

EURYDICE: Orpheus!

ORPHEUS *(talking in his sleep):* Do you love that man? I want to know if you love that man . . .

EURYDICE *(shaking him):* Orpheus . . .

ORPHEUS: What is it? Is it you?

He opens his eyes and turns around. At that moment the lights go out. The room is in total darkness.

EURYDICE: It's me, Eurydice . . . I know you often fall asleep with the light on, but as this power failure has lasted for at least an hour, I thought I'd take the opportunity to come down and get a book.

ORPHEUS: A book? To read in the dark?

EURYDICE: Well . . . that is to say . . .

The electricity returns. Eurydice is still leaning over the bed, Orpheus is facing the wall.

ORPHEUS: Oh! Just think how dangerous it is to be so careless. Go back up and close the trap door. You gave me a terrible scare.

EURYDICE: Do you forgive me?

ORPHEUS: Yes, of course I do. Now go upstairs and go back to sleep.

Eurydice climbs up to the bedroom.

THE AUTHOR'S VOICE: A brief power failure prevented her from achieving her aim. She had to go on living. The next day . . .

The garage. Day.

Orpheus is in the car listening to a message on the radio. Heurtebise enters and walks over to the car.

ORPHEUS: Do you understand these signals?

HEURTEBISE *(listening):* Those are quotations from the Stock Market.

ORPHEUS *(changing stations; sound of Morse code):* And this?

HEURTEBISE: Be careful, your wife is coming.

ORPHEUS: Again!

HEURTEBISE: Don't push her too far.

EURYDICE *(behind the door):* May I come in?

HEURTEBISE *(to Orpheus):* Close your eyes a minute. *(shouting)* Yes, come in!

Eurydice enters and walks over to the car.

HEURTEBISE: Your husband is listening to the Stock Market report. Get in the back of the car.

Heurtebise opens the back door. Eurydice gets in. Sound of the radio. Heurtebise gets in next to Eurydice. She is sitting directly behind Orpheus.

EURYDICE: Am I disturbing you?

ORPHEUS: I came here to get out of your way in the house.

EURYDICE: That sound is frightening.

She moves closer to Orpheus until her cheek touches his.

HEURTEBISE: Don't do anything careless, will you?

EURYDICE: Careless? Orpheus can't see me, yet I can touch his cheek. Isn't that marvelous?

Orpheus is fiddling with the radio knob. Suddenly it speaks.

THE RADIO: . . . are twenty-two. Three times. Two and two are twenty-two. Three times . . .

Orpheus looks up. His eyes fall on the rear-view mirror. He sees Eurydice. She vanishes.

HEURTEBISE *(shouting):* The mirror!

ORPHEUS *(shouting):* Eurydice!

Orpheus and Heurtebise get out of the car. Sound of drums.

HEURTEBISE: It was fatal.

ORPHEUS: It had to be! It had to be, Heurtebise! I was sick to death of compromises and settlements. One cannot compromise, Heurtebise. One must live fully, one must go to the end of things!

Sound of drums and chanting "Cegestius! Cegestius!" Orpheus rushes to the door.

HEURTEBISE *(trying to restrain him):* Orpheus! Orpheus!

The garden.

Orpheus runs out into the garden. Sound of people banging and knocking on the garden gate. Stones fall around Orpheus. The windows shatter.

ORPHEUS *(shouting at Heurtebise):* Stones! Stones! They can build my statue with them.

HEURTEBISE *(rushing to the garden gate):* Don't stay out there!

The stones are still falling all around them. Orpheus flattens himself against the wall next to Heurtebise.

ORPHEUS: Here they are! I was expecting them, the bastards! The letter, Heurtebise! The anonymous letter!

The road.

Shouts of "Cegestius! Cegestius! Cegestius!" A crowd of young people are shouting and throwing stones.

The garden.

HEURTEBISE: I'll go and talk to them.

ORPHEUS: What does marble think when it is being sculpted into a masterpiece? It thinks, "They're ruining me! They're destroying me! They're insulting me!" I'm ruined! Life is sculpting me, Heurtebise, allow it to complete its task.

Heurtebise runs toward the garage.

The garage.

Heurtebise takes a revolver out of the car and loads it.

The garden.

Heurtebise gives Orpheus the gun.

ORPHEUS: The cowards!

HEURTEBISE: Threaten them with the gun. It's your home!

The road.

The Bacchantes arrive in a large car. They incite the crowd by shouting: "The wall! Climb over the wall!"

The garden gate.

The young people climb over the wall and open the gate. The first person in the group comes forward. The drums become silent. Orpheus faces them with the gun in his hand.

FIRST WRITER: Give me that revolver. I order you to give me that revolver.

ORPHEUS: And I order you to leave the premises. I forbid you to enter my home.

FIRST WRITER: I shall do as I please.

ORPHEUS: Do you want to kill me?

FIRST WRITER: We want to know the whereabouts of Jacques Cegestius. Is he in your house?

ORPHEUS: One step and I'll shoot . . . I'll shoot . . .

A Chinese man grabs Orpheus' arm and twists it. The gun goes off and falls to the ground. A young man picks it up. Orpheus breaks away and punches him on the chin. He staggers. The gun goes off again. Orpheus clutches his stomach and collapses. The young people flee. The drums start up again.

The road.

Whistles. Drums. Shouts. The sound of motors. Shouts of "The police! The police! Get out of here!" The Bacchantes' car.

AGLAONICE *(standing):* Get going! Get going! Hurry!

People climb up onto the cars. They drive off. A police wagon stops in front of the gate. Roar of the motorcycles.

The garden.

The motorcyclists drive through the gate and wheel around. The police run in after them.

The road.

The police push the struggling young people into the wagon.

The garden.

The first motorcyclist and Heurtebise drag Orpheus' body into the garage. The second motorcyclist stays at the gate, fending off the police with a machine gun.

THE POLICE: Get away from that gate!

SECOND MOTORCYCLIST: We're taking care of a wounded man. Just keep calm and we won't harm you.

The road.

The police struggle with the crowd of young people, hitting them with clubs. Sound of a car engine. The garden gate opens and Heurtebise backs the Rolls onto the road at top speed, turns it around, and drives away. The two motorcyclists roar off behind him. The police run out onto the road and shoot at them. The sound of whistles, drums, and motors continues.

Viaduct on a deserted road.

The Rolls comes to a halt halfway across the viaduct. The motorcycles are on each side of the car. One of the motorcyclists comes up to Heurtebise.

FIRST MOTORCYCLIST: Hello. Everything all right?

HEURTEBISE: Everything's all right.

Heurtebise turns around. Orpheus' eyes are blank; his head is thrown back in a position confirming death.

The car drives off.

The chalet.

Night. Sound of drums. Orpheus climbs up the stairs like a sleepwalker. Heurtebise is behind Orpheus and pushes him with his hands on his shoulders. Their feet disappear down the steps that lead to the room with the mirror.

The Zone.

The ruins of the steps. Sound of drums.

The Princess and Cegestius are waiting, standing exactly as they had been at the close of the Tribunal. The Princess is dressed in black, her hair is loose. The drums die down.

PRINCESS: Cegestius . . .

CEGESTIUS: Madam?

PRINCESS: For once, I almost have the feeling of time. It must be terrible for men to have to wait . . .

CEGESTIUS: I don't remember.

PRINCESS: Are you bored?

CEGESTIUS: What's that?

Silence.

PRINCESS: Nothing. I was talking to myself.

The Zone. Arcades. The drums start up again.

Orpheus and Heurtebise walk flattened against the wall. They drag themselves along the wall by their hands, giving the impression they are crawling along the ground, flat on their stomachs. They pass an old woman who is huddled in a niche in the wall.

THE AUTHOR'S VOICE: It is not the same journey as before. Heurtebise is taking Orpheus to a forbidden place. He no longer walks upright and still. Orpheus and his guide drag themselves along, at times swept along on a strange wind, at times struggling against it.

Orpheus and Heurtebise slide down a steep slope. They seem to be flying along. Orpheus falls down at the bottom of the wall and drags himself away. Heurtebise follows him.

The drums stop. Music. The ruined steps. The Princess and Cegestius appear.

CEGESTIUS: They're coming . . .

The Princess rushes away to the right, leaving Cegestius standing behind her. The Princess and Orpheus come together at the arcades in the wall.

Music. Close-up of their faces touching. They murmur.

PRINCESS: Orpheus!

ORPHEUS: I found the way to join you.

PRINCESS: I cried out silently till you came.

ORPHEUS: I heard you . . . I waited . . .

PRINCESS: I didn't want you to stay in the world of men . . .

ORPHEUS: Where can we hide?

PRINCESS: We don't have to hide any more. We shall be free.

ORPHEUS: Forever . . .

PRINCESS: Forever. Hold me tight Orpheus. Hold me tight . . .

ORPHEUS: You are burning me like ice.

PRINCESS: I can still feel your human warmth; it's good.

ORPHEUS: I love you.

PRINCESS: I love you. Will you obey me?

ORPHEUS: I will obey you.

PRINCESS: Whatever I may ask?

ORPHEUS: Whatever you may ask.

PRINCESS: Even if I condemn you, if I torture you?

ORPHEUS: I belong to you and I'll never leave you.

PRINCESS: Never.

She moves away from Orpheus and turns to Heurtebise.

PRINCESS: Heurtebise, you know what I expect of you, don't you?

HEURTEBISE: But . . . Madam . . .

PRINCESS: It's our last chance. And we don't have a moment to lose.

HEURTEBISE: Think again . . .

PRINCESS: One mustn't think, Heurtebise!

HEURTEBISE: There is no crime as serious as this, in any world.

PRINCESS: Are you a coward?

AUTHOR'S VOICE: The Death of the Poet must sacrifice herself to make him immortal.

PRINCESS *(turning back to Orpheus):* Orpheus, I must ask you once and for all not to attempt to understand what I'm about to do. Indeed it would be very difficult to understand even in our world.

HEURTEBISE *(pushing Orpheus against the wall):* Stay there.

He positions him like a prisoner about to be shot.

PRINCESS: Quick . . . quick *(calling)* Cegestius! To work!

Heurtebise comes up behind Orpheus, puts one hand over his eyes, the other over his mouth. Cegestius runs up and holds Orpheus' legs against the wall. Together, they prevent him from moving. Orpheus tries to struggle.

PRINCESS *(shouting):* Orpheus, don't move! Keep still! You promised.

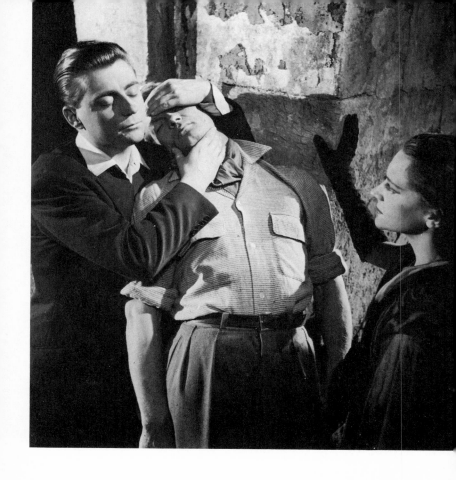

Orpheus gives in. The Princess walks up to the group and stands next to them against the wall.

PRINCESS: Work! Work! I'm helping you! I'm working with you. Don't give up. Count, calculate, make a supreme effort, as I'm doing. Come on, get him through the wall. You must! Without will power we are nothing. Come on . . . come on . . . come on! . . .

HEURTEBISE *(in a distant voice):* I can't . . .

PRINCESS: You must, Heurtebise, you must!

She stamps her foot.

HEURTEBISE: I can't . . .

He lets go of Orpheus' eyes and mouth. Orpheus' head falls back, as though he were asleep.

PRINCESS: You're not trying hard enough! Don't talk any more! Concentrate! Detach yourselves! Run! Run! Fly! Overcome all obstacles!

Orpheus stands as though asleep, with his head thrown back on Heurtebise's shoulder. Cegestius is huddled motionless against Orpheus' legs. The Princess comes up to them.

PRINCESS: You're getting near! You're almost there! I can see it!

HEURTEBISE *(in a distant voice):* I'm there . . .

PRINCESS: One last effort, Heurtebise. Go on! Go on! Are you there? Answer me. Are you there?

The Princess' face appears against the wall next to Orpheus'.

PRINCESS: Are you there?

HEURTEBISE *(in a distant voice):* Yes, I'm there.

PRINCESS: Well then, let's go! We must go back in time. What has happened must be wiped out.

(The action in the following scene is depicted through reversed film.)

It gets dark. Orpheus walks backward. Heurtebise holds him by the hand. They pass the glassmaker. Suddenly Heurtebise puts his hand to his forehead and stops. Orpheus stops too.

The Zone. The Princess, Heurtebise, Orpheus, Cegestius.

HEURTEBISE *(in a distant voice):* I'm so tired.

PRINCESS: I don't care. Work! Work! I command you.

(The action is again depicted through reversed film.)

Heurtebise and Orpheus disappear along the road amongst the ruins.

The room in the chalet.

They come through the mirror into the room.

The Zone.

PRINCESS: Where are you?

HEURTEBISE: In the room . . .

PRINCESS: The gloves, quick, the gloves.

Orpheus' bedroom.

The clock chimes six o'clock. Orpheus takes off the gloves and throws them to Heurtebise, who puts them in his pocket. Orpheus leaves; Heurtebise remains.

EURYDICE'S VOICE: Were you watching me sleep?

ORPHEUS' VOICE: Yes, my darling.

Eurydice and Orpheus are in each other's arms. Orpheus is kneeling beside the bed.

EURYDICE: I had the most terrible nightmare . . .

ORPHEUS: Do you feel ill?

EURYDICE: No, I just have a slight headache.

ORPHEUS *(kissing her):* I'll make you well.

As they talk, Heurtebise stands in the middle of the room.

EURYDICE'S VOICE: Were you working?

ORPHEUS' VOICE: Yes, I was working.

EURYDICE'S VOICE: You work too hard; you should rest.

ORPHEUS' VOICE: My books won't write themselves, you know.

EURYDICE'S VOICE: Your books do write themselves.

ORPHEUS: I help them. How's my son?

EURYDICE: Orpheus, it may be a girl.

ORPHEUS: It's a boy.

EURYDICE: He's kicking me. He punches me, too.

ORPHEUS: He will be as unbearable as his father.

EURYDICE: You, unbearable?

They kiss, laughing.

ORPHEUS: Many people find me unbearable.

EURYDICE: You shouldn't complain, you are adored!

ORPHEUS: And hated.

Heurtebise looks at them for a moment, then vanishes near the mirror.

EURYDICE: That's just a form of love.

ORPHEUS: The only love that matters is ours . . .

The Zone.

Cegestius stands up as though he had just awakened. Orpheus has disappeared. Heurtebise puts his hands to his head.

PRINCESS: It's done?

HEURTEBISE: It's done.

Cegestius looks to his left. The two motorcyclists come forward through the rubble.

CEGESTIUS: Madam! Madam! Your assistants! Are they going to arrest you?

PRINCESS: Yes, Cegestius.

CEGESTIUS: Run!

PRINCESS *(very wearily):* Where to?

CEGESTIUS: Madam, when one is arrested here, what happens?

HEURTEBISE: It's not funny, I can assure you.

CEGESTIUS: It's not funny anywhere.

HEURTEBISE: Least of all here.

PRINCESS *(turning as she walks away):* Heurtebise!

HEURTEBISE *(coming to her side):* Madam?

PRINCESS: Thank you.

HEURTEBISE: It was nothing. We had to return them to their muddy waters.

The gloved hands of the motorcyclists come down on their shoulders.

PRINCESS: Farewell, Cegestius . . .

Drums are heard over the music. The group sets off. Cegestius, looking distressed, takes a step forward and watches them leave.

The Princess and Heurtebise, flanked by the motorcyclists, walk away into the distance. Their shadows move across the background.

As they disappear, the words "THE END" appear.

There are no symbols or messages in this film. Such works are unfashionable in the bad sense of the word. It is a realistic film, which expresses cinematically that which is truer than truth itself — a superior realism, the truth that Goethe opposes to reality, the truth that is the great conquest of the poets of our era.

ORPHEUS

In the film, Orpheus is not a great priest. He is a famous poet whose celebrity annoys what has come to be known as the avant-garde. In the film, the avant-garde play the role of the Bacchantes in the fable. Here, the Bacchantes are the members of a women's club where Eurydice worked as a waitress before marrying Orpheus. Orpheus forbids Eurydice to associate with them. She disobeys him, because Aglaonice, Queen of the Bacchantes, still has a great influence over her. Orpheus incorporates several themes: The theme summed-up in Mallarmé's lines: "And so it was that eternity finally changed him in himself."

The poet must die several times in order to be reborn.

Twenty years ago I developed this theme in *The Blood of a Poet*. But there I played it with one finger; in *Orpheus* I have orchestrated it.

The theme of inspiration: one should say expiration rather than inspiration. That which we call inspiration comes from within us, from the darkness of our own night, not from outside, from a different so-called divine night. Everything starts to go wrong when Orpheus ignores his own messages and agrees to accept messages coming from outside. Orpheus is tricked by the messages that come from Cegestius, not from the beyond. They are inspired by the B.B.C. broadcasts of the occupation.

Some of the sentences are real; for example, "The bird sings with its fingers" comes from a letter that Apollinaire wrote me.

Note that talking cars belong to modern mythology, a mythology of which we are unaware because we are actually living it.

The cars and modern clothes are there by poetic license, as a means of bringing an old myth closer to today's spectators.

The comic scene of the return home is an illustration of what men say when they love another woman: "I can't bear to look at my wife," or, "I can't stand the sight of her."

In the final scene the Princess, Heurtebise, and Cegestius set to work on Orpheus and put him to sleep, in the same way that the Neophytes of Tibet are put to sleep to enable them to travel through time. This can be interpreted as death inflicted on someone already dead, thereby giving him life again.

CEGESTIUS

Cegestius is sixteen years old. The avant-garde is infatuated with him for no apparent reason, as is often the case. He is an excessive drinker, and his insolence and bravado are pleasing. But as soon as he reaches the Zone, he becomes himself again: a shy, young boy, somewhat naive but very noble.

HEURTEBISE

Heurtebise is by no means an angel, as he is in the play, and as he is often made out to be. He is a young man in the service of one of the infinite satellites of death. He is only just recently dead. He tries several times to warn the others (theme of free will). For example, he tries to warn Orpheus of the harmful nature of the radio messages and to warn Eurydice of the coming accident on the road.

But the fate he tries to thwart by an act of free will is a fate created by the Princess. This is why the court of inquiry does not hold it against him.

Lies are no longer legal tender at the Tribunal, which is held at the Princess' chalet. The Princess and Heurtebise have to confess to the faintest shadow of emotion and admit that the human world to which they once belonged still has a hold over them.

The sentence, "We had to return them to their muddy waters," does not mean to their earthly love but, quite simply, "back to the world."

THE TRIBUNAL

The Tribunal is a Court of the Underworld and the judges play the role of examining magistrates at a trial — and much more than that!

EURYDICE

Eurydice is a very straightforward woman, a housewife who cannot be touched by anything that does not concern her home. She is quite impervious to mystery.

She endures all the hazards of the legend with total purity and one objective in mind: her love for her husband. This love alone wins her case and convinces the Princess to undertake the strange act in which the theme of immortality is expressed.

The poet's death is canceled in order to make him immortal.

Short scene in front of the mirror.

HEURTEBISE: Do you forgive me for what I said at the Tribunal?
EURYDICE: What was it you said? . . .
HEURTEBISE: Nothing, I'm sorry . . .

This scene proves that even Heurtebise is not fully aware of the extent of Eurydice's pureness.

THE PRINCESS

The Princess does not symbolize death because this film has no symbols. She no more stands for death than an air hostess represents an angel. She is the Death of Orpheus, just as she decides to be the Death of Cegestius and of Eurydice. We each possess our own death, who watches over us from the day we are born.

In a way, she plays the role of a guardian whose job is to watch over someone and who saves him at the price of their own destruction.

What kind of condemnation does she inflict upon herself? I don't know. It brings to mind the enigmas that puzzle entymologists:

the enigmas of the ant hill and the bee-hive. Her perogatives are very limited. She does not know what she is exposing herself to. The Princess' and Orpheus' love for each other illustrates the deep attraction that poets feel for all that exists beyond the world they inhabit. It also represents their determination to overcome the infirmity that cuts us off from a host of instincts. We are haunted by these instincts, yet we are unable to define or enact them.

While they are waiting in the Zone, the Princess asks Cegestius, "Are you bored?" and Cegestius replies, "What's that?" The Princess' reponse, "Nothing, I was talking to myself," is an admission that questioning Cegestius is a pretext for questioning herself and her memories.

THE ZONE

The Zone has nothing to do with any dogma whatsoever. It is the fringe of life itself, a no-man's land between life and death. There, one is neither completely dead nor completely alive. The glassmaker who walks past Heurtebise and Orpheus is a dead young man who insists on selling his wares in a place where windows no longer have any meaning.

Orpheus asks Heurtebise; "Who are all these people wandering around? Are they alive?" Heurtebise replies, "They think they are; there is nothing so stubborn as professional enthusiasm."

THE MIRRORS

I almost forgot the theme of the mirrors. They show us growing older and bring us closer to death.

I have presented the outlines of the film, in which all the themes are intertwined, from the Orphean myth, itself, to more contemporary ones.

The film does not pretend, however, to be more than a paraphrase of an ancient Greek legend, which is quite natural since time is a purely human notion and, in fact, does not exist at all.

La Belle et la Bête   *(1946)*

Credits

Screenplay	Jean Cocteau (from the fable of Madame Leprince de Beaumont
Director	Jean Cocteau
Producer	André Paulvé
Music	Georges Auric. Conducted by Roger Desormières
Technical Adviser	René Clément
Décor	René Moulaert and Carré
Costumes	Designed by Escoffier and Castillo for the Maison Paquin
Cameramen	Henri Alekan
	Henri Tiquet
	Foucard
	Letouzey
	Aldo
Make-up	Arakelian
Continuity	Lucile Costa
Editor	Claude Iberia
Assistant Director	Roger Rogelys
Assistant Producer	Emile Darbon

Cast:

Avenant, The Beast, The Prince	Jean Marais
Beauty	Josette Day
Felicie	Mila Parely
Adelaide	Nane Germon
Ludovic	Michel Auclair
The Merchant	Marcel André

Children have implicit faith in what we tell them. They believe that the plucking of a rose can bring disaster to a family, that the hands of a half-human beast begin to smoke after he has killed, and that the beast is put to shame when a young girl comes to live in his house. They believe a host of other simple things.

I ask you to have the same kind of simple faith, and, for the spell to work, let me just say four magic words, the true "Open Sesame" of childhood:

"Once upon a time . . . ."

JEAN COCTEAU.

Beauty lives in the country with her father, a 17th-century merchant who has lost all his money; her brother, Ludovic, whose only interests are drinking and gambling; and her two sisters, Felicie and Adelaide, who are motivated entirely by spite, selfishness and vanity. Her brother's constant companion, Avenant, is a frequent visitor to the house.

Ludovic and Avenant are shooting arrows at a target fixed onto the wall of the house.

Felicie and Adelaide are inside.

FELICIE *(angrily):* Oh, that wretched girl!

ADELAIDE: You know she can't do anything right.

LUDOVIC *(taking aim and shooting):* A bad one.

He steps aside. Avenant aims.

LUDOVIC: Your foot.

AVENANT: What about my foot?

LUDOVIC: You're cheating, it's not on the mark.

Avenant shoots. The arrow flies straight through the upper window of the house and impales itself in the floor next to a silk cushion. A little dog leaps up from the cushion, barking furiously. Beauty is attending to her sisters who, in sharp contrast to her simple attire, are dressed in rich silks and feathers.

FELICIE: What's going on?

ADELAIDE: They've just shot an arrow into the room!

FELICIE: Oh!

ADELAIDE *(going to the window and shouting):* You hooligans! You could have hit one of us in the eye!

Ludovic and Avenant rush up to the house.

AVENANT: Is Beauty all right?

ADELAIDE *(shouting out of the window):* Beauty! Always Beauty! Who cares about Beauty? You nearly killed Cabriole!

Ludovic and Avenant go into the house and wait at the foot of the stairs.

LUDOVIC *(ironically):* Here they come.

Felicie and Adelaide hurry down.

FELICIE *(shouting):* Beauty, you can wash the floor. We'll be late for the duchess.

ADELAIDE *(to the two men):* Murderers!

LUDOVIC *(to Avenant):* My sisters are such bitches.

FELICIE *(to Adelaide):* Drinking, chasing women and cheating at cards, that's all they ever think about. They couldn't give a damn about anything else.

LUDOVIC *(to Avenant):* When one is poor, one stays at home to do the laundry and polish the pots and pans. Just look at these two sluts — they think they're princesses. They don't even realize that they're the laughing stock of society.

ADELAIDE *(to Felicie):* Say something!

FELICIE: He'd be only too pleased.

They flounce out of the house.

LUDOVIC: Oh, such beauties! So ravishing!

ADELAIDE *(to Felicie):* Come on, we'll be late for the concert.

LUDOVIC *(following them out of the house):* Enchantresses! Goddesses! Shining lights!

FELICIE *(shouting):* Hey there! Boys! Boys!

LUDOVIC *(imitating her):* Boys! Boys!

Felicie and Adelaide walk across the yard toward a servant who is dozing in a sedan chair.

ADELAIDE: Oh!

The boy leaps out of the chair. Felicie sits down.

FELICIE *(angrily):* This is unbelieveable!

Adelaide walks over to another servant who is lolling against a pile of straw.

ADELAIDE: I suppose you think we pay you to sleep!

She walks over to a second sedan chair.

ADELAIDE *(angrily):* I've never seen anything like it!

She opens the door to the chair. Three or four hens cackle and flap their wings as she shoos them out of the chair.

ADELAIDE: Oh, the chairs. *(She sits down.)* Look at them, they're filthy! Boys! Boys!

Two more servant boys come running out of the stable.

ONE OF THE BOYS *(yawning):* Come on, let's go.

FELICIE: Stop dawdling, wake up now!. . . You've been drinking!

The four boys pick up the two sedan chairs and stumble their way across the yard. They pass in front of Ludovic, who is leaning against the wall, watching in amusement.

ADELAIDE *(to Felicie):* Just look at this drunkard. He doesn't even know his proper role in society.

FELICIE: A barefoot guttersnipe!

The boy carrying her sedan chair kicks open the gate, jolting the chair as he maneuvers it through.

FELICIE: Yes, they're drunk, drunk!

ADELAIDE: Come along, come along now! Oh, boys, careful!

Ludovic comes up behind them and watches them leave.

LUDOVIC: May the devil splash you with mud and cover you in dung!

Back at the house, Beauty is polishing the floor in her sisters' room. Avenant comes up to her and plucks the arrow from the floor.

AVENANT *(kneeling down beside her):* Beauty, you were not made to be a servant. *(He points to the shining floorboards.)* Even the floor would like to mirror you. *(He pulls her to her feet.)* You can't go on working from morning to night for your sisters.

BEAUTY: If our father's ship hadn't got lost in the storm, then perhaps I'd be able to enjoy myself as they do. But we're ruined, Avenant, so I must work.

AVENANT: I wonder why your sisters never do any work.

BEAUTY: My sisters are too beautiful, their hands are too white.

AVENANT: Beauty, you are the most beautiful of them all. *(He takes her hands.)* Look at your hands.

BEAUTY *(trying to free herself):* Let go of my hands, Avenant. Leave, so that I can finish my work.

AVENANT: I love you. Marry me.

BEAUTY: No, Avenant, don't talk to me of marriage; it's useless.

AVENANT: I displease you.

BEAUTY: No, you don't, Avenant.

AVENANT: Well then?

BEAUTY: I must stay single and live with my father.

She turns away and walks toward the door. Avenant runs after her and takes hold of her.

AVENANT: Beauty, I shall snatch you away from this senseless existence!

BEAUTY *(struggling):* Leave me alone!

LUDOVIC *(bursting into the room):* Take your hands off her, or I'll smash your face in!

BEAUTY: It's all right, Ludovic. Avenant was asking me to marry him.

LUDOVIC: And what was your reply?

AVENANT: Your sister has rejected me.

LUDOVIC: Well done, Beauty. I know I'm a scoundrel and even proud of it, but I won't have you marry one. *(He walks over to Avenant.)* And you can take that as final. Go on, you louse, get out of here!

Avenant strikes him. Ludovic staggers and falls over.

BEAUTY *(running over to him):* Avenant! You're crazy! Ludovic! Ludovic!

Downstairs, the merchant enters the house, ushering three men in before him.

THE MERCHANT: Come in, gentlemen, come in. I want you to feel part of the family when I announce the great news. *(He shows them to a table.)* Gentlemen.

They all sit down.

BEAUTY *(from the top of the stairs):* It's my father! *(She turns to the others.)* He must know nothing of this!

THE MERCHANT *(bringing refreshments to the table):* My daughters are out enjoying the flattery of society life. I shan't wait for them. I just can't hold my tongue any longer.

Beauty, Ludovic and Avenant come down the stairs into the room.

THE MERCHANT: Come here next to me, Beauty. Come closer Ludovic. You too, Avenant, you're most welcome. These gentlemen are willing to forgive you for all your pranks. And the Public Prosecutor has very generously decided to drop the charges he was going to bring against me. We're going to be rich! One of my ships has come into port!

LUDOVIC *(angrily):* Avenant must have known!

AVENANT *(protesting):* Ludovic!

LUDOVIC: He knew! And he took advantage of it to ask Beauty to marry him!

BEAUTY: That wasn't the first time he's asked me to marry him since we lost all our money.

THE MERCHANT *(to Beauty):* So you want to leave me.

BEAUTY: No, father, I'll never leave you.

Felicie and Adelaide burst into the room.

FELICIE: We were told that the duchess was not receiving, though the court rang with laughter and music. *(angrily)* Let me congratulate you, father, we are gathering the fruits of your foolish deeds.

ADELAIDE: Yes, you can feel proud of yourself.

FELICIE: And here you are entertaining people with drinks, while your daughters are insulted and doors are slammed in their faces!

THE MERCHANT: Children! Children!

LUDOVIC: The duchess would appear to be a most admirable woman.

ADELAIDE: I nearly died of shame!

FELICIE: Come on, Adelaide, let them drink to our misfortunes.

They flounce out of the room.

BEAUTY: Oh father, father.

THE MERCHANT: They're real little devils, aren't they. Let them sulk; I'll soon console them. Tomorrow morning I'll go to the port to see to my business. Then one can marry a duke and the other a prince! *(He raises his glass in a toast.)* Gentlemen!

The following morning.

The merchant is on his way out of the house.

FELICIE: Bring us back brocade dresses.

ADELAIDE: And jewels, fans and ostrich feathers.

FELICIE: I want the whole town to burst with envy! A monkey! I'd like a monkey!

ADELAIDE: A parrot!

The merchant laughs and mounts his horse.

THE MERCHANT *(turning to Beauty):* What about you? Beauty, what shall I bring you?

BEAUTY: Father, bring me a rose, for they don't grow here.

Adelaide and Felicie burst out laughing.

Later.

Ludovic and Avenant are seated at the table drinking. They are waiting for the usurer.

LUDOVIC: If I don't pay off my debt tonight I shall be arrested and thrown in jail.

AVENANT: The moneylender is very understanding. I explained the whole situation to him. Look confident, here he comes.

THE USURER *(entering the house):* You're asking for a very large sum, you know, very large. . .

AVENANT: You do know that one of the lost ships has come into port, don't you?

LUDOVIC: I'll pay you back as soon as my father returns.

THE USURER: You know the law, don't you. If you're insolvent, I can

claim the sum of money from your father and if he's insolvent I
can seize his furniture.

AVENANT *(to Ludovic):* Sign, you're not risking anything, are you?

The usurer gives him a document. Ludovic signs.

In town. A lawyer's office.

THE LAWYER: But my dear Sir, what can I do?

THE MERCHANT *(in despair):* As there's nothing left from this last
ship, what's to become of me?

THE LAWYER: Your creditors at the port moved faster than the ones
in town. Sue them.

THE MERCHANT: Sue them! I haven't even got enough to pay for a
room tonight.

THE LAWYER: Well, go home then.

THE MERCHANT: But I'll have to go through the forest in the middle
of the night. I'll get lost.

THE LAWYER: You came through it at night on your way here, didn't
you?

THE MERCHANT: Yes, but there was a full moon then, and it's getting
foggy now. I know I'll get lost.

THE LAWYER *(losing his patience):* Well then, get lost.

The lawyer shows him out.

THE MERCHANT: I don't understand you; I'm sure you'd feel the
same if you were in my shoes. It's very frightening.

THE LAWYER: Good night!

The merchant fetches his horse, mounts and starts off.

THE LAWYER: Good luck!

The merchant rides deeper into the forest. It grows dark and a storm breaks. After a while he realizes that he has lost his way. He dismounts and leads his horse along the narrow forest paths, peering anxiously through the thickening mist. During a flash of lightning through the leaves he suddenly sees a magnificent castle. With a puzzled look on his face he walks slowly through the trees across a courtyard toward the castle gates. As he makes his way, the branches silently close in behind him. When he reaches the gates, they open before him. Surprised, he lets go of the horse's reins. The horse walks in ahead of him. The merchant follows, but the gates close in front of him. He runs back across the courtyard and looks up at the castle.

The castle.

THE MERCHANT: Is there anyone there?

In front of him is a wide stone staircase leading to a door in the castle's wall.

THE MERCHANT *(running up the stairs):* Is there anyone there?

He goes through the door and is confronted by a row of human arms holding candelabras, showing him the way down a corridor to a large hall. He stops and stares in disbelief. Two of the human arms release the candelabras, which remain magically suspended, pointing toward the hall. Awed, the merchant backs into the room toward a huge fireplace. A clock on the mantlepiece strikes eleven. He turns around and looks from the fire to a dining table, which is sumptuously set with food and drink.

THE MERCHANT: Is there anyone there?

He puts his hat on the table, sits down and removes his gloves. A marble bust, which supports one end of the vast mantlepiece, slowly turns its head toward him. At the other side of the fireplace, its counterpart, breathing smoke through its nostrils, also moves its head around to look at him.

The merchant reaches for a silver goblet. A hand appears from the candelabra in the middle of the table. The merchant starts back. The hand takes hold of a wine decanter, fills the goblet, and returns to the candelabra. The merchant lifts up the edge of the tablecloth and peers underneath it. He stares at the candelabra on the table, stands up and turns to look once more at the row of candelabras leading out of the room.

He sits down again, picks up the goblet, sniffs at it suspiciously, and drinks. He falls into a deep sleep. The marble busts turn their heads again.

The merchant slowly wakes up. His hand is resting on the wooden arm of his chair, which is carved in the image of a lion's head. The lion's head comes to life under his hand and roars.

The merchant leaps to his feet and grabs his gloves. The marble bust breathes smoke. The candelabra on the dining table extinguishes itself.

The merchant takes a last look around the room, walks hurriedly down the corridor past the row of candelabras and leaves the castle. The door shuts silently behind him. He walks slowly down the stairs and along a balustrade decorated with stone statues of fierce-looking dogs. He stops and looks around him.

THE MERCHANT: Hey there!

ECHO: 'Hey there!'

THE MERCHANT *(walking along the balustrade)*: Hey there!

ECHO: 'Hey there!'

THE MERCHANT *(coming to the end of the balustrade)*: Hey there!

ECHO: 'Hey there!'

He goes down some steps and finds himself in a beautiful rose garden. He looks around nervously and walks over toward the flowers. Suddenly he stumbles over the body of a dead deer.

THE MERCHANT *(starting back with a look of horror)*: Hey there!

He looks down and sees a perfect rose, which changes color as he watches. Just as the merchant plucks the rose, the Beast appears through a curtain of leaves.

THE BEAST: Hey there!

The Beast walks over to the merchant. He has the appearance of a werewolf, with long fangs and grotesque features. His huge gnarled hands end in claws and, like the rest of him, are covered in thick matted fur. He is wearing a long jeweled cloak over a doublet with slashed sleeves and a broad lace collar, a pair of velvet breeches and high leather boots.

As he speaks, the wind blows and the leaves and branches rustle.

THE BEAST: So, my dear Sir, you steal my roses. My roses which are the most precious things in the whole world to me. You are most unfortunate since you could have taken anything but my roses. The penalty for such a simple theft is death.

THE MERCHANT *(flinging himself to his knees)*: My Lord, I did not know. I did not think I would offend anyone by plucking a rose for my daughter. She asked for one.

THE BEAST: One does not call me "my Lord"; one calls me "Beast." I don't like compliments. No, don't try to understand. You have fifteen minutes in which to prepare yourself for your death.

THE MERCHANT: My Lord!

THE BEAST *(angrily):* Again! The Beast orders you to be silent. You stole my rose and you shall die. Unless . . . . . . unless one of your daughters . . . . How many do you have?

THE MERCHANT: Three.

THE BEAST: Unless one of your daughters agrees to pay the penalty and take your place.

THE MERCHANT: But. . .

THE BEAST *(angrily):* Don't argue! Go! Take advantage of the one chance I have given you. And if your daughters refuse to die instead of you, swear that you'll return in three day's time. Swear!

THE MERCHANT: I swear. But I don't know my way through the forest. . .

THE BEAST: You'll find a white horse in my stables. His name is 'Magnificent One.' Just whisper in his ear, "Go where I am going, Magnificent One, go, go." He'll take you home and lead you back to the castle if your daughters are too cowardly to mount him. Now leave.

The Beast backs away into the curtain of leaves and disappears. The merchant runs off toward the stables. A beautiful white stallion awaits him there. He mounts him and sets off.

As the white horse carries the merchant through the forest, the Beast watches him through the leaves. The branches close in silently behind the merchant as he makes his way home.

Later.

The merchant is at home, surrounded by his family.

THE MERCHANT: I can't tell you anything about my journey home. The Magnificent One is in the stable. That's the end of my story. Beauty, take this rose, I'm paying a high price for it.

FELICIE: That's what happens when an idiotic girl asks for roses. This is the result of that silly creature's vanity.

ADELAIDE: And she pretends to be modest, and set us an example. She's not even crying.

BEAUTY: You won't die, father. It's my fault; it's only right that I go in your place.

AVENANT: Are you mad? We'll go with Ludovic and we'll kill this horrible beast.

THE MERCHANT: The Beast is so powerful that we have no hope of overcoming him. Don't worry Beauty, I'm growing old. I promised, so I shall go.

FELICIE: You mustn't go, father, you may yet win your case.

ADELAIDE: How will we live?

THE MERCHANT: You can sell the furniture.

LUDOVIC: Why don't you go, Felicie? You're too tough for anyone to eat!

FELICIE: It's a great pity that the Beast isn't demanding boys. He would devour you and die of poison!

THE MERCHANT: Children, keep calm. . .

BEAUTY: Father, I'd rather be devoured by the monster than die of the heartbreak of losing you.

AVENANT: You will not go to the monster.

FELICIE *(angrily):* What's it got to do with you?

AVENANT: It's none of your business!

FELICIE: Are you in love with that stupid girl? What a couple!

LUDOVIC: Avenant, hit her.

THE MERCHANT: Keep calm, please. . .

AVENANT: Go on, repeat what you just said!

FELICIE: A stupid girl and a stupid boy!

Avenant hits her.

FELICIE: He hit me!

LUDOVIC *(angrily):* You dared to strike my sister!

AVENANT *(to Ludovic):* There's more where that one came from. . .

ADELAIDE: You villain!

THE MERCHANT *(in a faltering voice):* Children . . . children. . .

BEAUTY: He's unwell.

AVENANT: Let's carry him to his room.

Avenant and Ludovic help him out.

FELICIE *(angrily):* He hit me, Adelaide.

ADELAIDE: And we're penniless.

FELICIE: We mustn't give up.

ADELAIDE: The Beast will gobble them all up, and we'll marry princes.

Meanwhile, Beauty comes out of the side of the house, wearing a long dark cloak. Making sure that no one sees her, she goes to the stable and mounts the white horse.

BEAUTY: Go where I'm going, Magnificent One, go, go!

The horse trots out of the stable. The farm gates open before him. He carries Beauty through the forest to the castle. She dismounts and leads him through the foliage, which closes in behind her.

As though in a dream she enters the castle and floats past the rows of candelabras, through the large hall with the fireplace, and up a flight of stairs. She goes through a door which leads to a long gallery with billowing white curtains. Seemingly carried along by some magical force, she comes to a door flanked on each side by human arms carrying candelabras. The arms move toward the door, casting their light onto her.

VOICE *(whispering as the door opens):* Beauty, I am the door to your room.

Beauty enters the room hesitantly. The door closes silently behind

her. She looks round the room which is spacious, elegantly fur-
nished, and full of flowers and plants. A marble bust on one of the
walls moves its head around toward her.

Beauty rushes over to the open window as though seeking her
freedom. Realizing the futility of her action, she sits down at a
dressing table and, in despair, puts her head in her hands.

VOICE FROM THE DRESSING TABLE MIRROR *(whispering):* Beauty, I
   am your mirror; reflect in me; I will reflect for you.

Beauty puts her hands out toward the mirror and gazes into it. The
glass is black. Then she sees her father lying on his sickbed. The
mirror turns black again. She stands up and looks round the room.
On the large bed, a luxurious fur cover is pulled back by invisible
hands. Beauty runs out of the room, along the corridor, out of the
castle, down the stone staircase into the courtyard.

Across the courtyard the doors open and the Beast makes his
appearance. Beauty lets out a cry of fear and horror.

THE BEAST: Where are you going?

She falls to the ground in a faint. The Beast walks over to her,
gathers her gently in his arms and carries her carefully up the stone
staircase with a look of anguish mingled with tenderness.

He takes her back into the castle, past the row of candelabras, up the
stairs into her room. As he crosses the threshold of the room,
Beauty's clothes are transformed. She is dressed like a princess in a
richly embroidered silk dress with sparkling jewels. The Beast puts
her down gently onto the bed and stares at her intently. She
awakens, opens her eyes, and turns her head toward the Beast. As
she sees him she lets out a cry. He backs away across the room.

THE BEAST: Beauty, you mustn't look me in the eyes. Do not fear,
   you will never see me, except every evening at seven, when you
   dine. I shall come to the great hall. *(He backs out of the room.)*
   You mustn't look me in the eyes.

The door closes silently behind him.

In the great hall the clock strikes seven. On each side of the blazing fire the marble busts turn their heads. Beauty is sitting at the table, wearing a dark jeweled dress, with matching jewels round her neck and wound into her hair. The hand from the candelabra on the table picks up the silver wine decanter to serve her. She leans back in her chair with a sigh of despair and closes her eyes. The door opens behind her and the Beast crosses the room. He stands behind her, leaning on the back of the chair.

THE BEAST: Don't be afraid.

BEAUTY *(summoning up all her courage):* I . . . I won't be afraid.

THE BEAST: Beauty, do you mind if I watch you while you dine?

BEAUTY: You are the master.

THE BEAST: No, I'm not. *(He pauses for a moment.)* There is no master here but you. *(He moves around to the side of the chair.)* I revolt you; you must find me very ugly.

BEAUTY: I cannot lie, Beast.

THE BEAST: Is everything here to your liking?

BEAUTY: I feel uneasy dressed in such finery, nor am I used to being waited upon. But I know you're doing your utmost to help me forget your ugliness.

THE BEAST *(walking over to the fireplace):* My heart is kind, but I am a monster.

BEAUTY: Many men are more monstrous than you, but they hide it well.

THE BEAST: Besides my ugliness, I am lacking in wit.

BEAUTY: You have wit enough to realize it.

THE BEAST: Everything in this castle is yours. Your every whim will be fulfilled.

THE BEAST *(walking back to the dining table):* I shall appear every evening at seven. Before leaving I shall ask you a question; it will always be the same one.

BEAUTY: What is your question?

THE BEAST: Beauty, will you be my wife?

BEAUTY: No, Beast.

THE BEAST: Farewell then, Beauty. Until tomorrow.

He leaves the room.

Later.

Beauty walks fearfully across the hall. She is wearing a long white silk gown. She hears a sound like the roar of wild beasts followed by the screams of an animal in pain. She walks along the gallery, keeping close to the wall as though looking for protection. The white curtains billow in the breeze. She stops by a marble bust, aware of some presence. The Beast appears and walks past with a look of hideous despair. He doesn't see her hidden behind the statue. He stares at his huge grotesque hands, the sharp claws, and buries his head in his arms. Beauty watches him in horror. He turns, goes to the door of her room, leans against it for a moment with the same look of anguish. He enters the room, searching desperately for her. He sits down at the dressing table, picks up the mirror and gazes into it.

THE BEAST: Where is Beauty? *(shouting)* Where is Beauty?

Smoke billows out of the mirror. He gazes into it and sees her edging her way slowly along the gallery to the door, listening carefully for any sound from within. The Beast puts down the mirror, stands up and looks at the door.

Beauty enters the room.

BEAUTY *(angrily):* What are you doing in my room?

THE BEAST *(meekly):* I wanted to . . . I was . . . I came to your room to bring you a gift.

He holds out his hand. A pearl necklace magically appears in the palm of his hand.

BEAUTY *(shouting):* Leave!

She runs out of the room. Disconsolately, the Beast puts the necklace down on the dressing table.

BEAUTY *(in a softer voice):* Leave.

The Beast walks slowly out of the room.

Beauty walks across the room to the dressing table and picks up the pearl necklace. She looks at it pensively.

Later.

Beauty is walking through the castle grounds. She comes to a door. She pushes it open and looks through onto a pool of water surrounded by plants and trees. The Beast is on his knees by the edge of the pool, lapping up the water like an animal. Beauty closes the door and backs away with a concerned look on her face. She continues her walk through the grounds. She is wearing the pearl necklace that the Beast left in her room. The Beast appears among the stone statues of dogs.

THE BEAST: I thought you were dining, Beauty.

BEAUTY: I'm not hungry, Beast. I'd prefer to walk with you.

THE BEAST *(in a gentle voice):* Beauty, you're doing me a great honor . . . *(They walk side by side along the stone balustrade.)* . . . a very great honor.

BEAUTY: Your voice seems gentler.

They stop.

THE BEAST: Beauty, I hope you don't find the days too tedious.

BEAUTY *(walking on):* I do find the days long. And this evening I admit I was almost looking forward to seven o'clock.

THE BEAST: You are so kind that I can hardly bring myself to ask you the question which torments me so.

BEAUTY: Ask, I shall always give the same reply. Let's be friends, Beast, don't ask any more of me.

They walk on through the grounds.

BEAUTY: Tell me, Beast, how do you pass the day?

A deer leaps through the bushes. The Beast stares at it greedily as it runs away into the woods.

BEAUTY: Did you hear me, Beast? I'm talking to you.

THE BEAST *(in a troubled voice):* For . . . forgive me.

BEAUTY *(putting her hand on the Beast's arm):* Beast! What is it?

The Beast puts his head in his hands and turns away in shame.

THE BEAST: Forgive me, please forgive me, it's nothing.

Beauty hesitantly puts out her hand. He takes it, and leads her down the stone staircase. They come to a fountain. The Beast puts his head in his hands again.

BEAUTY: What's the matter, Beast?

THE BEAST: I'm thirsty, Beauty.

Beauty goes to the fountain and fills her hands with water.

BEAUTY *(holding out her hands):* Drink from my hands.

The Beast laps the water from her hands and stares at her intently.

THE BEAST: Doesn't it revolt you to give me drink?

BEAUTY *(looking him straight in the eyes):* No, Beast, it gives me pleasure. I would never wish to cause you any pain.

THE BEAST: And yet your dream is to be far away from me.

Beauty is in the great hall, walking up and down in front of the fire. She is wearing a dark velvet dress. The marble busts at each end of the mantlepiece turn their heads to watch her. The clock strikes half past seven. Beauty looks up at the clock and sees the Beast's reflection in the mirror above it. She turns round as he walks across the room.

BEAUTY: How late you are!

THE BEAST: Thank you, Beauty, for noticing.

BEAUTY: Yes, I was awaiting you with great impatience, Beast. *(She throws herself to her knees and grabs his cloak.)* I must talk to you!

THE BEAST *(shocked):* Beauty! Beauty!

BEAUTY *(still on her knees, pleading):* I cannot live another day without seeing my father again. Please let me go, I beg you!

THE BEAST: Stand up, Beauty, stand up.

He pulls her to her feet and leads her to a chair. He sits down beside her.

THE BEAST: I should be on my knees taking orders from you.

BEAUTY *(almost in tears):* Let me go. I promise to return.

THE BEAST: And when you return, will you be my wife?

BEAUTY *(in despair):* You're torturing me.

THE BEAST: I know I'm repulsive. But I would die of heartbreak if I let you go and you took advantage of your freedom never to return.

BEAUTY: I'd come back in a week's time. I respect you too much to cause your death. .

The Beast lowers his head. Beauty strokes it.

THE BEAST *(looking up at her):* You coax me as though I were an animal.

BEAUTY *(gently):* But you are an animal.

THE BEAST: Your request is a very serious matter. I must think about it. *(He stands up.)* Beauty, will you come into the garden with me?

He takes her hand and leads her out of the castle.

THE BEAST: Beauty, has someone already asked for your hand in marriage?

BEAUTY: Yes, Beast.

THE BEAST: Ah! . . . And . . . who asked for your hand? A young man?

BEAUTY: Yes, Beast.

THE BEAST: Is he handsome?

BEAUTY: Yes, Beast.

THE BEAST: Why did you not marry him?

BEAUTY: I didn't want to leave my father.

THE BEAST: And what is this handsome young man's name, Beauty?

BEAUTY: Avenant.

The Beast looks at her, turns away as though in pain and suddenly runs away through the trees.

BEAUTY *(shouting):* Beast! What's the matter? . . . Beast! Beast! What is it? . . . Beast!

Later.

Beauty is lying in bed. Suddenly she hears a noise outside the door. She runs to the door which opens before her. The Beast is standing in the shadows.

BEAUTY: What are you doing at my door at such a late hour?

The Beast moves into the light.

BEAUTY: My God! You're covered in blood!

She starts back in horror.

THE BEAST: Forgive me . . .

BEAUTY: For what?

THE BEAST *(almost groveling):* For being a beast, forgive me.

BEAUTY *(firmly):* It doesn't become you to talk in that way. Aren't you ashamed of yourself? Go and clean yourself and go to sleep.

She stands there looking at him in all her innocence and purity. The Beast is overcome with shame and self-disgust.

THE BEAST *(in despair):* Close the door! Close the door! *(She doesn't move.)* Quick . . . quick, close the door. Your look is burning me, I can't bear it.

He backs away. The door closes silently behind him. Beauty walks slowly toward the bed with a troubled look on her face.

Later.

At the merchant's house.

The bailiffs are removing the furniture on instructions from the usurer. Avenant and Ludovic are sitting at the table, watching.

AVENANT: They're taking every single thing.

LUDOVIC: I don't suppose they'll even leave the table.

AVENANT: Let's play cards.

He picks up a pack of cards. The usurer walks over to them with a disapproving look.

THE USURER *(to Ludovic):* Go up to your father. He doesn't understand what's going on, which is only natural. I can't very well explain the situation to him.

Ludovic looks doubtfully at Avenant.

AVENANT *(resigned):* Go on.

Later.

Upstairs the merchant is lying ill in bed. Ludovic stands beside him, looking sorry for himself.

THE MERCHANT *(in a weak voice):* Ludovic . . . Ludovic . . . is it true?

LUDOVIC: I'm afraid it is.

THE MERCHANT: Ludovic, how could you have done such a thing!

The usurer hurries into the room.

AVENANT *(following him):* Sir, he's a very sick man, you must leave the bed.

THE USURER: Yes, yes, we won't take the beds.

They go downstairs into the hall. Adelaide and Felicie run down the stairs and hurry out of the house.

LUDOVIC: I bet they've seen to it that no one touches their things!

THE USURER: No, no, they too owe me money.

THE BAILIFFS *(coming through the door with more furniture):* Come on, it's all got to go!

The usurer leaves the house. Avenant and Ludovic sit down at the table in the otherwise bare room. Ludovic brings out a purse and pours money onto the table with a smile. Avenant picks up the pack of cards and deals. Ludovic looks at his hand.

LUDOVIC *(piling up his stake):* A pair!

AVENANT *(throwing down a card):* Ace!

LUDOVIC: Oh, I nearly had you.

AVENANT *(laughing):* That's not good enough!

LUDOVIC *(picking up the cards and shuffling them):* My deal.

The usurer bursts into the house.

THE USURER *(angrily):* You cheats! Give me my money!

He tries to pick up the money from the table. Ludovic strikes him and knocks him out.

LUDOVIC: What shall we do?

AVENANT: Throw him out. The streets are empty at this time of night.

LUDOVIC: What time is it? Wait a minute.

He leans down and takes the watch and chain off the usurer's frock coat. He looks at it.

LUDOVIC *(grinning):* Ten o'clock.

He puts the watch inside his jacket.

At the castle.

The Beast watches the whole scene in the mirror in Beauty's room. Beauty is lying on the bed. The Beast walks over to the foot of the bed.

THE BEAST: Beauty, are you ill?

BEAUTY: Yes, Beast, I am.

THE BEAST: What ails you?

BEAUTY: I know my father's dying.

THE BEAST: I can't bear to see you waste away.

BEAUTY: Send me home to my father.

THE BEAST: If I agree, will you promise to return in a week's time, to the very day?

BEAUTY *(smiling at him):* I promise.

THE BEAST *(going to the edge of the bed and putting out his hand):* Come with me, Beauty. *(He helps her down from the bed and leads her through the French windows out onto the balcony.)* Look over there, Beauty. *(He points to an ornately decorated small pavilion.)* You see that pavilion? It's called the pavilion of Diana. It's the only part of my domain where no one may enter. Not even you or I. Everything I possess, I possess by magic powers. But my true riches lie locked in that pavilion. A golden key opens the door. Here it is ... *(He shows her the key.)* Beauty, I couldn't give you greater proof of my faith in you. If you don't return I shall die. After my death, you risk nothing more and all my riches will be yours. Take this key, Beauty. *(He hands it to her.)* I have faith in you. The key will be your pledge to return.

BEAUTY *(looking at him with an expression of joy):* You agree to send me home to my father?

THE BEAST: You'll be there this very morning. My night here is not the same as yours. It is night in my world, but it is morning in yours. *(He leads her back into the room.)* Beauty, a rose that has already played its part, my mirror, my golden key, my horse and my glove are the five secrets of my power ... I surrender them to you. *(He removes his glove and gives it to her.)* Just put the glove on your right hand, it will carry you wherever you wish. *(He walks slowly to the door, turns round and looks at her intently.)* Remember your promise. *(The door opens; he leaves the room.)* Farewell, Beauty.

The door closes silently behind him. Beauty paces up and down the room, staring at the glove. She puts it onto her right hand. In a flash she is transported to her father's bedroom.

The merchant is sleeping. Beauty throws the glove onto the bed and sits down. Gently, she puts her hand out toward him. He wakes up.

THE MERCHANT: I must be dreaming!

BEAUTY: No, father, you're not dreaming. It is I, Beauty, talking to you.

THE MERCHANT: I thought you were dead, and it was killing me. But you managed to escape?

BEAUTY: No, father, the Beast set me free to visit you.

THE MERCHANT: So the monster has a heart.

BEAUTY: He suffers greatly, father. One half of him is in constant struggle with the other. I think he is more cruel to himself than he is to others.

THE MERCHANT: But Beauty, I've seen him, he's so hideous.

BEAUTY: Yes, at first he's very frightening, father. Yet now, he sometimes makes me want to burst out laughing. But then I see his eyes, and they're so sad that I turn away so as not to weep.

THE MERCHANT: Beauty, my little Beauty, don't tell me that you're willing to live with this monster!

BEAUTY: I must father. Certain powers obey him, but others control him. If I escaped I'd be committing a crime against him and against you.

THE MERCHANT: Does he threaten you?

BEAUTY: He only comes to me when his cruelty need not be feared. Sometimes his bearing is regal, but sometimes he almost limps, as though he were the victim of some terrible affliction.

THE MERCHANT: How can you feel sorry for him?

BEAUTY: I can bear his presence because I would be happy if I could make him forget his ugliness.

THE MERCHANT: Beauty . . . Beauty, you're paying a high price for being so good.

BEAUTY: But father, the monster is good.

A tear falls from her eyes onto her hand. It is magically transformed into a diamond.

THE MERCHANT: Good God! A diamond!

He picks it up, looks at her, and puts his hand to her cheek where another tear glistens.

THE MERCHANT: Another one!

BEAUTY: It is proof that he is protected, for I wept thinking of him.

THE MERCHANT: Maybe the devil sent these diamonds!

BEAUTY: Rest assured, father, keep them. They are a gift from him. Now you'll be able to support yourself. But if you tell my sisters of this miracle, they'll take them from you and you'll have nothing.

Later.

Outside in the yard, Felicie and Adelaide are hanging up the washing. They are dressed in peasant clothes. Ludovic is feeding the chickens.

FELICIE: I'd rather lie on the sheets than have to hang them up. My hands are in the most dreadful state!

LUDOVIC *(ironically):* How appalling.

ADELAIDE: Look at mine! A kitchen maid! That's what I've been reduced to!

LUDOVIC: Well, my lovely princesses, when one is penniless, one has to work!

FELICIE: You fool!

ADELAIDE *(to Ludovic):* Yes, you can talk, you good-for-nothing. If we hadn't lost all the furniture, we'd still have a maid.

Avenant is chopping wood across the yard.

AVENANT *(joining them):* It's all my fault. And you may have noticed that I'm paying for it now.

ADELAIDE: Yes, when you're not drinking or gambling.

AVENANT: Oh, you're so charming. *(He pauses.)* How was your father this morning?

LUDOVIC: As if they cared! I'm the only one that looks after him. He's still very weak. He can't get up.

Suddenly they hear the merchant shouting in a strong voice.

THE MERCHANT: Felicie! Adelaide! Ludovic!

Felicie climbs up onto a stool and peers out over the line of washing.

FELICIE: Well, I never! A lady from the court, walking with my father!

ADELAIDE: And here we are dressed in rags!

AVENANT: It's Beauty!

LUDOVIC: Beauty! It can't be!

ADELAIDE: It is!

The merchant and Beauty walk across the yard. Beauty looks like a princess. She is wearing a long white silk dress with full sleeves and a low-cut neckline. Her hair flows down her back in elaborate curls, and on her head she wears a jeweled coronet from which floats a

translucent pearl-studded train. Her only piece of jewelry is a magnificent pearl necklace with a diamond clasp. The two sisters stare at her in disbelief. Avenant helps Felicie down off the stool.

FELICIE: Leave me alone, will you!

AVENANT: You become sweeter by the moment.

THE MERCHANT: Beauty came to my room and cured me.

LUDOVIC: Where have you come from?

FELICIE *(staring greedily at Beauty's necklace):* What a magnificent necklace!

BEAUTY *(removing it and offering it to her):* Take it, Felicie, it will look even better on you.

Felicie grabs it eagerly. It turns into a bunch of dirty twisted rags.

THE MERCHANT: My God!

ADELAIDE: Put it down!

FELICIE: How disgusting!

She drops it. As it touches the ground it turns back into pearls. The merchant picks up the necklace and puts it on Beauty.

THE MERCHANT: What the Beast gave you is for you alone. You can't give it away.

FELICIE *(angrily):* Come on Adelaide, let's go and get dressed. We must look simply ghastly.

LUDOVIC: Good-bye, you sweet young things!

The two sisters stalk out of the yard.

BEAUTY *(looking at the washing on the line):* Who did my washing?

AVENANT: We did!

BEAUTY: The sheets are badly hung, they're trailing on the ground.

LUDOVIC: So, this Beast wasn't savage?

BEAUTY: No, Ludovic, he's a good beast.

AVENANT: You're not going back to him, are you?

BEAUTY: I must, Avenant, I promised. The Beast set me free for one week, and if I don't return he'll die of heartbreak.

AVENANT *(angrily):* Do you love him?

BEAUTY: No, Avenant, I'm fond of him. It's not the same thing.

Inside the house the two sisters are dressing.

ADELAIDE: The Church Committee would be most interested in that little exhibition of witchcraft we've just witnessed.

In the yard.

THE MERCHANT *(kissing Beauty on the cheek):* I'll see you later.

He leaves.

LUDOVIC: Let's go to the stable. We can talk seriously there. My dear sisters won't be able to hear us.

They walk across the yard and go into the stable.

LUDOVIC: Tell us everything.

BEAUTY *(sitting down on a wooden bench):* He gave me the key to all his treasures. He trusts me implicitly. I'd be the monster if I didn't return to him.

LUDOVIC: What about your servants? Are there many?

BEAUTY: Invisible hands serve me, dress me, arrange my hair, open and close the doors. I never see anyone.

AVENANT: And this Beast speaks like a human being?

BEAUTY: Yes, Avenant, he speaks just like you and I do.

LUDOVIC: Does he crawl on all fours? What does he drink? What does he eat?

BEAUTY: Sometimes I help him drink — and I know he'll never eat me.

Inside the house. The two sisters are dressed up in all their finery.

FELICIE: Well, I never!

ADELAIDE: It's incredible!

FELICIE: That little fool is happier than we are — and she's rich. After all, so many husbands are no better than her Beast.

ADELAIDE: She's bursting with pride!

FELICIE: Don't worry, I've got a good head on my shoulders. We must be very friendly and let the boys worm out her secrets.

Later.

Downstairs. Avenant and Ludovic are sitting at the table. Ludovic empties his pockets.

AVENANT: Show me how much you've got.

LUDOVIC *(throwing a coin onto the table):* There you are. It's pretty bad.

AVENANT: We must do something. I've come to a decision.

LUDOVIC: There's nothing we can do.

AVENANT: Ludovic, the idea of Beauty returning to that Beast tomorrow is intolerable. We must slay the Beast.

LUDOVIC: And take his treasure! But do you appreciate the power of magic?

AVENANT: I don't believe in magic. I'm sure the monster hypnotizes

Beauty and makes her believe anything he wants her to.

LUDOVIC: I'm scared.

AVENANT: When it comes to rescuing Beauty no magic power in the world could scare me. Anyway we have no choice. So don't be ridiculous. Butter up your sisters — when they see what's in it for them, they'll stop Beauty from leaving. Tempt them with the promise of riches.

LUDOVIC: And by what miracle will you find the Beast?

AVENANT: I'll question Beauty and find out her secret.

Later.

In the kitchen.

FELICIE: We'll rub our eyes with onions and pretend to cry.

ADELAIDE *(holding up an onion):* She'll smell it. Ludovic's ideas are ludicrous.

FELICIE: She's too stupid to notice. Ludovic's idea isn't all that silly. Leave it to me. *(She hands the onion to Adelaide who rubs it in Felicie's face.)* Charming! . . . Go on . . . go on . . .

They run into Beauty's room, holding handkerchiefs to their faces. Beauty is wearing her simple peasant clothes.

FELICIE *(dramatically):* Beauty, you can't leave us, you mustn't go!

ADELAIDE *(flinging herself to her knees at Beauty's feet):* Beauty, stay with us!

FELICIE: I know we have been unfair to you, but at the thought of losing you we realize just how much we love you!

BEAUTY: You're crying!

FELICIE *(pretending to sob):* If the Beast loves you, he won't mind if you stay a little longer.

ADELAIDE: Stay another week!

BEAUTY: It's not possible.

FELICIE: Do you want us to die of heartbreak? Your father? Your sisters? Stay . . . Stay, Beauty . . . Stay with us!

BEAUTY *(turning away):* I can't.

FELICIE: Don't be cruel. Stay!

Adelaide pretends to sob hysterically.

BEAUTY *(stroking her forehead):* Adelaide, Adelaide! My dear sister.

FELICIE: Adelaide said to me, "We have got our dear Beauty back. I shall die if she leaves!"

BEAUTY: Don't tempt me.

ADELAIDE: Beauty!

FELICIE: Don't abandon us tomorrow. Tell the Beast that it was your sisters' fault.

She turns away in false despair and walks over to the dressing table. She sees the golden key lying there and snatches it while no one is looking.

BEAUTY *(sighing):* I didn't realize that you were so fond of me.

FELICIE *(smiling falsely):* You're an angel.

She runs up to Beauty and embraces her.

ADELAIDE *(kissing her):* We're so happy! So happy!

Beauty throws herself onto the bed in despair. The sisters leave the room.

ADELAIDE: Oh, I'm so happy!

Felicie closes the door behind her and listens.

FELICIE: She's crying!

ADELAIDE: She'll stay behind, and we'll share all the treasure!

FELICIE: Let's wash our faces. You stink!

They go downstairs. Ludovic is waiting for them.

LUDOVIC: Well?

FELICIE: Well what?

LUDOVIC: Is she staying?

FELICIE: She's staying.

LUDOVIC: Did you get the key?

FELICIE: Look! *(She opens her hand.)*

LUDOVIC: Give it to me.

FELICIE *(putting her hand behind her back)*: What do you take me for?

ADELAIDE *(to Ludovic)*: Who knows what you'd do with it; it's solid gold, you know.

LUDOVIC: You stupid fool.

FELICIE: Don't start fighting. I'll give it to Avenant — if he decides to go.

LUDOVIC: Oh, women! You really are incredible! Typical. Go how? Go where?

FELICIE *(shrugging her shoulders)*: Avenant will just have to find a way.

Later.

The family is dining.

THE MERCHANT: Beauty, you seem so sad.

BEAUTY: No, I'm not, father.

FELICIE: She misses her luxuries. Our wretched way of life upsets her.

THE MERCHANT *(angrily):* Felicie! Felicie!

ADELAIDE: The Beast must have certain attractions that we don't possess.

Beauty gets up to serve the wine.

THE MERCHANT: Oh!

FELICIE: Doubtless Madam feels that it's beneath her to wait on us.

Beauty runs out of the room.

THE MERCHANT: Beauty! Beauty!

She goes outside with her head in her hands, sobbing.

AVENANT *(coming up to her):* What have they done to you now? It's your sisters, isn't it? They didn't wait long! Damn it! Beauty,

listen to me, don't cry. I must wake you from this nightmare. I must take you away. I know what you're thinking — that I'm a good-for-nothing. But with you beside me, I'd work. We'd leave the town and its taverns behind us. Answer me. *(She is silent.)* What is it? I see, it's the Beast. Tell me how to get to him, I'll go and kill him. *(He pauses.)* You don't answer. I was sure of it; the Beast has bewitched you or at least you can't bring yourself to wish him harm. *(Beauty listens to him with tears in her eyes.)* Well, Beauty, let me tell you — that monster can't be suffering as I do or he would fly to you and make you follow him. Rest assured, Beauty, he has forgotten you.

She shakes her head and leaves him.

Later. At the castle.

The Beast is pacing up and down in Beauty's room. He looks at his bare right hand in despair. He goes over to the dressing table and fingers the mirror. He walks slowly round the room and stares at the empty bed. He picks up the fur bedspread and strokes it, as he holds it to his cheek and clutches it to his breast with a look of anguish.

Later.

At the merchant's house. The stable.

Felicie opens the door to let in Avenant and Ludovic.

FELICIE: Come in, no one will find us here.

ADELAIDE: You're late, of course.

FELICIE: Well?

AVENANT: I have reached a decision. There's no looking back now!

LUDOVIC: That's all very well, but how can we get to the Beast?

FELICIE: Didn't you find out how Beauty got here?

AVENANT: Beauty only tells us what the Beast has allowed her to tell. We know every detail about the domain, but she won't say anymore.

FELICIE: To hell with her; if she won't tell, I'll torture her till she does!

AVENANT: If you do that, don't count on any more help from me! *(They hear a sound.)* What's that? I'll go and see.

He goes to the door. The Magnificent One trots into the yard.

AVENANT: A riderless white horse! It's the Magnificent One, I'm sure. He jumped over the gate and came into the yard.

FELICIE: Heaven sent him!

LUDOVIC: More likely Hell.

ADELAIDE: I'm scared!

FELICIE: Shut up, you fool. Avenant, open the door quietly and bring him in.

AVENANT: Don't move, I'll go.

He goes out into the yard and leads the horse into the stable.

FELICIE: The Beast has sent him for Beauty. What luck. Avenant, the horse can take you and Ludovic to the domain.

LUDOVIC: It's easy for you to talk!

FELICIE: Are you a man, or aren't you?

AVENANT: We mustn't waste a second. *(He mounts the horse.)* Come on, Ludovic, jump up behind me.

LUDOVIC *(getting up behind him):* May God protect us.

FELICIE *(picking up their bows and arrows):* Your bows!

She hands them to Avenant. He looks down. Something is hanging from the saddle.

AVENANT: What's that?

FELICIE: It's a bag. If it were gold, I'd only have to touch it and it would turn to straw. *(to Adelaide)* Open it.

ADELAIDE *(looking inside the bag):* A mirror!

She takes it out. It's the mirror from Beauty's room in the castle.

FELICIE: His message to her is clear: Look and you will see the ugly face of a girl who breaks her promises.

LUDOVIC: You see, the Beast's not all that stupid after all.

FELICIE *(giving Avenant the key):* Here's the key — off you go, and good luck!

AVENANT: I've forgotten the magic words.

LUDOVIC: It's something like "Go, go."

FELICIE: If I depended on you we'd get nowhere! Go where I am going, Magnificent One, go, go.

AVENANT: Go where I am going, Magnificent One, go, go.

The horse neighs and gallops out of the yard.

ADELAIDE *(running after them):* Ludovic!

FELICIE: What's the matter?

ADELAIDE: Suppose we've sent them to their death . . .

FELICIE: Don't be stupid. *(They go into the house.)* The mirror!

ADELAIDE: I don't feel happy about it.

FELICIE *(holding up the mirror):* Look at you, green with fear.

Adelaide lets out a cry of horror. The mirror reflects the cruel and ugly face of an old hag.

ADELAIDE: Look!

She holds the mirror up to Felicie. Felicie looks into it and sees an ape.

FELICIE: Oh!

ADELAIDE: What can you see?

FELICIE: Nothing. Let's take it to Beauty, it's her turn.

They go to Beauty's room. She is wearing the fabulous clothes and jewels that she had on when she arrived.

FELICIE: Ah! So Madam dolls herself up like a princess when she's alone in her room.

ADELAIDE: Yes, just who do you think you are?

FELICIE: Here, Beauty, here's a mirror that was mysteriously left at the door for you. *(She throws it on the bed.)* To show you how a Beauty must look to please a Beast.

They leave the room.

Beauty goes over to the bed and picks up the mirror. She holds it to her cheek and props it up on the dressing table. She lies down on the bed and gazes into it. At first she sees her own reflection. Then the Beast appears to her, with a look of intense suffering. The mirror goes black. Beauty lies back on the bed in despair. Suddenly she sits up. She looks at the mirror again, hurriedly picks up the Beast's glove which is lying next to it and puts it on her right hand.

She is transported to her bed in the castle. She removes the glove and sits up.

BEAUTY: Oh! the key! *(She puts the glove on again.)*

She is taken back to the house. She removes the glove and looks round the room for the key.

BEAUTY: The key! *(desperately)* Where is the key? My God!

She throws herself onto the bed and hurriedly puts on the glove again.

Back in her room in the castle, she rushes to the door which opens silently before her.

BEAUTY: Beast! My Beast! *(She runs out of the castle, down the stone staircase. She stops and searches in vain for the Beast.)* Beast! *(in despair)* Beast! *(She runs through the garden shouting for him. Suddenly she sees him lying on the ground by the edge of the pool.)* My Beast! *(She runs to his side and kneels over him.)* My Beast, answer me, Beast! Oh, my Beast, forgive me! *(She tries to lift up his head.)* Answer me, Beast. Look at me. Your glove will revive you. *(She puts it on his right hand.)* Help me! *(She looks at him.)* I'm the monster, Beast. You shall live, you shall live!

THE BEAST *(whispering):* It's too late.

Meanwhile, Avenant and Ludovic have reached the pavilion.

LUDOVIC: We're here!

AVENANT: Yes, we're here. First we must kill the Beast.

LUDOVIC: We'll kill him later. Have you got the key?

Avenant brings out the key and is about to put it into the lock.

LUDOVIC: Wait! This key may release some evil trap. We must be very careful.

AVENANT: You're right. We won't go in through the door. Follow me.

They walk round the side of the pavilion. The walls are covered in plants. Avenant tests the branches.

AVENANT: Climb up after me. *(Ludovic hesitates.)* Come on, take heart. You're scared of course.

LUDOVIC: I'm not scared, I'm thinking.

AVENANT: It looks the same to me. Are you coming?

LUDOVIC *(following him up onto the roof):* Where are we?

AVENANT: We're on a skylight. *(He pulls back the foliage and peers down into the pavilion.)* Look!

They gaze down at innumerable jewels, gold and other treasures piled up around a statue in the middle of the pavilion.

LUDOVIC: It's fantastic! *(He points to the statue.)* What's that?

AVENANT: The goddess Diana.

Meanwhile, Beauty is still desperately trying to revive the Beast.

BEAUTY: You're no coward, I know the strength of your claws. Clutch at life with them, fight! Sit up, roar, frighten death away!

THE BEAST: Beauty, if I were a man . . . doubtless I would . . . do as you say . . . but poor beasts who would prove their love . . . only know . . . how to lie on the ground . . . and die.

He gives her a look full of tenderness and dies.

On the roof of the pavilion Avenant is spurred into action by the sight of the Beast's treasure.

AVENANT: I'm going to break the pane. *(Ludovic tries to hold him back.)* Leave me alone! *(He breaks the glass with the heel of his boot.)* After all, it's only glass. You hold me by the arms, and lower me down as far as possible, then I'll jump.

LUDOVIC: It's too high.

AVENANT: I'll jump.

LUDOVIC: How will we get the treasure out?

AVENANT: We'll think of something. First we've got to get in there. Stand square on your feet. *(Ludovic takes hold of his arms.)* Get a good grip.

Ludovic lowers Avenant down through the skylight. The statue of Diana comes to life, puts an arrow in her bow and aims at Avenant.

AVENANT: Wait, wait Ludovic, don't let go yet. Wait until I tell you to.

Diana shoots the arrow. It hits Avenant between his shoulder blades. He lets out a cry. Ludovic stares at him in horror. Before his very eyes Avenant's features turn into those of the Beast. Ludovic lets go of him, he falls to the ground — there is no sign of the treasure, only dead leaves and branches.

At the edge of the pool Beauty starts back with a cry.

BEAUTY: Where is the Beast?

A handsome young man stands in front of her.

THE PRINCE: The Beast is no more. It was I, Beauty. My parents wouldn't believe in fairy tales. The fairies punished them — through me. I could only be saved by a look of love.

BEAUTY *(amazed):* Are such miracles possible?

THE PRINCE: We are the proof. Love can make a Beast of a man. It can also make an ugly man handsome. *(She looks away.)* What is it Beauty? Do you regret my ugliness?

BEAUTY: No, my Lord. You resemble someone I once knew.

THE PRINCE: Who?

BEAUTY: My brother's friend.

THE PRINCE: You loved him?

BEAUTY: Yes.

THE PRINCE: Did he know?

BEAUTY: No.

THE PRINCE: But you loved the Beast?

BEAUTY: Yes, I did.

THE PRINCE: You are a strange girl, Beauty, a strange girl indeed.

BEAUTY *(kneeling at his feet):* I am at your service.

THE PRINCE *(lifting her to her feet):* Does my resemblance to your brother's friend displease you?

BEAUTY *(turning away):* Yes . . . *(She turns back to him and smiles.)* No.

THE PRINCE *(taking her in his arms):* The first time I carried you in my arms I was the Beast . . . *(In the pavilion the remains of the Beast lie smoking on the ground.)* Are you happy?

BEAUTY: I shall have to get accustomed to you. Where will you take me?

THE PRINCE: To my kingdom, where you will be Queen. There you'll find your father, and your sisters will carry your train.

BEAUTY: Is it far?

THE PRINCE: We'll fly through the air. *(He picks her up in his arms.)* You won't be afraid, will you?

BEAUTY: I don't mind being afraid . . . with you.

He carries her out into the courtyard. In the pavilion dead leaves flutter onto the remains of the Beast. The Prince kisses Beauty's hand.

THE PRINCE: Beauty! I will take you! Come, away!

Hand in hand they are magically carried aloft through the clouds into the sky.

The End